RAWHIDE STORM

Rawhide had a long account to settle with Dean Saxby. Framed by him on a murder charge, it was only by luck that he hadn't hanged for it. Now he had got out of the penitentiary to find that Saxby had run off with his wife and sold up his ranch. Between Rawhide and Saxby was the terrible Journada del Muerte — a vast expanse of sand and snakes. But it didn't deter Rawhide Storm, and the score was soon going to be settled.

Books by Mark Donovan
in the Linford Western Library:

RATTLESNAKE RAILROAD
THIRD MAN'S RANGE

MARK DONOVAN

RAWHIDE STORM

Complete and Unabridged

LINFORD
Leicester

First published in Great Britain

First Linford Edition
published October 1995

British Library CIP Data

Donovan, Mark
Rawhide storm.—Large print ed.—
Linford western library
I. Title II. Series
823.914 [F]

ISBN 0–7089–7762–6

Published by
F. A. Thorpe (Publishing) Ltd.
Anstey, Leicestershire
Set by Words & Graphics Ltd.
Anstey, Leicestershire
Printed and bound in Great Britain by
T. J. Press (Padstow) Ltd., Padstow, Cornwall

This book is printed on acid-free paper

1

"STORM! hey, Storm! C'mon, git up outa that bunk! C'mon, you're wanted — pronto! C'mon, or I'll beat you out!"

Storm smothered a groan, opened his puffed, swollen eyes, rolled painfully off the hard planks and lurched to the barred door of his cell where the warder impatiently waited, night stick poised, an expression of malign satisfaction on his coarse, battered face — "Boys shore gave you a workin' over las' time," he said as Storm sidled through the half open door, hands and arms wrapped protectively round his head — "Yeah, an' they'll do it again if you ain't quit bein' sassy."

Storm dropped his hands from his face, spoke slowly through his bruised lips. "I'll git even with you, Lacy, if it takes me for ever!"

Lacy laughed, a harsh, cruel cackle of a laugh — "It will, Storm, it will; time you've had put on your stretch for assaultin' guards you won't never git outa here alive. C'mon, git movin'! Governor wants you!"

As they moved through hall after hall, doors unlocked before and relocked behind them, Storm tried to flog his brain into some sort of activity, but brutal cruelty had so benumbed it he could think of no reason why the Governor should want to see him, nor could he come to any conclusion while he waited stiffly at attention while the hatchet-faced Governor wrote steadily for ten minutess in front of him before raising his inhuman, almost colourless eyes. Those eyes examined Storm incuriously, like a woman looking over potatoes, then a smile quirked the thin mouth. "It don' pay not to co-operate, huh? When you come in here I tol' you to play ball an' it ain't so bad. Wa'al, you played it different, so you hadda be taught."

Storm licked his lips. "I'm an innocent man," he croaked.

"That's what they all say," the Governor sneered. "Always some other jasper, but . . . " he paused, glanced down at a scrawled letter on his desk, "but as for you — seems like you tol' th' truth."

Storm blinked and tried to restrain the hope that leapt to his heart; four months in jail had taught him the bitter lesson that any betrayal of emotion could only lead him into worse trouble and more beatings up — "Nothin' to say, huh?" the Governor commented. "I got a letter here from Sheriff Bond who says he's turned up a witness as seen Denton shot — an' it wasn't you."

"So I'm free to go?"

The Governor's eyes narrowed. "Free from th' murder rap? — yeah. But don' go thinkin' you kin jus' walk outa here, Storm. You been a goddam nuisance to us, an' unless you're ready to sign a form sayin' you been treated

3

right — we'll keep you!"

Storm drew a deep breath. His brain was working again — and fast; there had been talk in the jail that the newspapers were raising a racket about the way prisoners were treated; he could tell the reporters a lot, enough to make the Governor's job unsafe. "Awright, I'll sign," he muttered. At that moment he would have done anything, absolutely anything to get out of jail, so badly had his spirit been broken by savage brutality.

The Governor's eyes met his. "Awright," he said, "an' don' forgit — one wrong word from you, Storm, an' I'll frame up a charge that'll bring you back here for life. Git me?"

Storm moistened his lips and scrawled his signature on the paper the Governor held out; for one fleeting moment he did wonder whether this was just one more attempt to trap him into an admission that he had killed Denton. But no, the Governor had been speaking the truth, and still more than half dazed Storm passed semi-consciously through the routine of release; he saw the prison doctor, who cynically told him, "You're in fine shape, feller, jail chuck shore agrees with you!" He got his own range clothes back and some of his personal belongings — those that had no value. Then, after what seemed an age, the gate clanged shut behind him and he was out in the sunglare of the dusty street, sustaining the curious stares of idlers who tilted their chairs back on the porch of the *Last Chance* saloon opposite, chewing and spitting rhythmically, occasionally exchanging laconic comments on the state of the world.

Storm moved uncertainly away from the gate, his high-heeled, thin-soled boots awkward after the heavy footgear issued to him in the jail; he felt his arm gripped and smelt again the stench of Lacy's foul breath.

"You ain't clear o' me yet," Lacy jeered. "Ain't you th' lucky feller? Red carpet an' all! Me an' Joe, we're gonna see you take th' train; Governor's a soft-hearted cuss, he's gonna pay yore fare an' all! Git movin, Storm!" This last was hardly an instruction Storm could ignore, for with Lacy holding one arm and Joe the other he was hurtled away upstreet towards the railroad depot; in some strange way that last insulting humiliation, coming on top of all else he had suffered, sufficed to break the spell of mute acceptance which had settled leadenly upon his spirit. In an instant rage seethed his brain and he knew he could not leave town before settling some of the debt he owed Lacy.

"How long before th' train?" he queried hoarsely, making an effort to keep his voice respectfully subservient.

"'Bout an hour."

"Shore could do with a drink," he suggested.

Lacy laughed. "Don' think we're gonna buy you one, do you?"

"I got some dinero," Storm admitted grudgingly.

"You? How?"

"That's my business."

Lacy stopped and wrenched Storm round to face him.

"You? Why, you two-timin' four-flusher! You been holdin' out on me all these months! I got a mind . . ."

"Hold it, Lacy," Joe warned. "'Member what th' Governor said — he don' want no fuss. If this punk's got cash we'll drink it. Sid's oughta be quiet now."

Lacy's hunched shoulders relaxed.

"Awright," he said, "but if you're crossin' us, Storm . . ." He let the words hang as they hurried Storm down a side street and into a saloon where the lonely barman dozed, his head on the counter. "Now let's see this cash," Lacy ordered. "Set 'em up, Sid. This punk's payin'." Storm bent to fumble in the lining of his right boot, then brought up a ten-spot; Lacy snatched it from his hand and slapped it on the bar.

"An' to think he had that all th'

time," he muttered, downing his first whisky and reaching for the bottle. Storm reached for his glass; he was icy cool, his brain working once more with some of the clarity which had been smothered in jail. He needed that drink, needed it badly to brace him for the dangerous moment to come; as he replaced it on the bar his hand swept down and plucked Lacy's gun neatly from the big man's holster.

"Now!" he gritted, as he moved lightly back a couple of paces. "Now I'm gonna git some o' my own back. You, Joe! Turn around, walk up to me. An', Sid, you keep yore han's away up — away from that scattergun!"

Dull-faced and bewildered, Joe did as he was told, backed up and had his gun taken. With a Colt in each hand Storm almost smiled at the rage in Lacy's eyes, rage in which there began to dawn a tinge of apprehension.

"You two buzzards had a lot o' fun beatin' me," Storm reminded them. "Now I'm gonna have a lot o' fun watchin' you beat each other! Git after it, fellers!"

"You gone jail crazy, Storm?" Lacy blustered roughly.

"I ain't," Storm told him succinctly. "I been roughed up by you two bastards often enough — I aim to get me some real fun watchin' you do to each other what you did to me. You . . . Joe, I've heard you call Lacy a misbegotten son of a mountain goat — an' that was on'y a start."

Lacy glowered at Joe. "I always knew you had it in for me. Was it you as tol' th' Deputy Governor about that . . . "

"That feller you killed an' then said he'd fell down th' stairs? It wasn't me, but I would ha' done!"

Storm backed gently away as the two big, tough warders grew redder and redder in the face and more and more violent in their language; had he but known, the two had long hated each other's guts, and only a doubt on Lacy's part as to whether he could whop Joe had prevented a clash long before; now he had to fight, so he started it by bringing up one knee hard into Joe's crotch. Joe part blocked the blow and swung a long, looping right that landed on Lacy's arm. The punch didn't knock Lacy down but put him off balance, and Joe got in two fast uppercuts before Lacy kicked him in the belly.

"They ain't so tough without night sticks, are they?" Sid the barman grinned to Storm; he was watching the fight with obvious enjoyment. "They been a dang nuisance in here, them two," he complained, "always pickin' quarrels with other hombres an' bustin' th' place up, never pay nothin' for breakages neither."

His face gashed and bleeding, Lacy backed away, then put his bullet head down and charged forward like a buffalo. Arms swinging hard, he bored in and brought his head sharply up against Joe's chin. Joe grunted with pain, lurched back against the bar as Lacy's hand clutched his throat. It was by no means a pretty fight; each man knew every dirty trick, learnt in a school where no trick was of any use unless it was designed to maim a man; they kicked and gouged and rabbit-punched, and it was a tribute to their toughness that it was some three minutes before the savage punishment each absorbed was sufficient to put one of them down — that was Lacy, floored by a haymaker that could have left few teeth in his mouth. Instantly Joe jumped on him, then kicked viciously at his jaw. Lacy groaned once and lay still except for the jerks his body gave as Joe went on kicking him. Joe went on kicking until Storm felt sick, sick in spite of the treatment Lacy had meted out to him. He flipped out one Colt and struck hard and accurately at the base of Joe's neck, after which the other jailer collapsed.

Sid rubbed his hands slowly together, his eyes sparkling. "Gee, that was worth plenty," he said, "an', feller, I enjoyed it — th' which same you ain't gonna when them two wake up — they'll frame you soon's bat an eye. Goin' far?"

"Hawksbee — by railroad!"

"They'd use th' wire — you wouldn't have a chance. Lookit, I got me a cayuse out back, took it for a bad debt an' don' hardly ever use it. Take it an' welcome."

"But I ain't got th' price . . . "

"Nuts! You gimme th' best fun I had in years, an' that hayburner's eatin' holes in my pocket. C'mon, git movin', feller, you better git outa town pronto — an' don' argyfy!"

★ ★ ★

Five minutes later Storm left the town at a fast trot; he was riding a hammer-headed claybank horse with a wicked-tempered eye and powerful quarters; the animal clearly hadn't been ridden much recently and Storm, after his months in jail, had some difficulty in sticking in the saddle and justifying his nickname of Rawhide! He quietened the horse before he was far down street and few people noticed him in his faded range clothes and well-worn chaps, a tall, stringy man with a face burnt mahogany brown by long years in the saddle — even then he hadn't quite acquired the jail pallor; he was a man with a bitter twist to his mouth and a faraway, untrusting look in his grey eyes, a man who looked as if he'd be a good friend but a hard, unrelenting enemy; his eyes were bleak and sombre as they glared warily about from under his battered Stetson, a man a little puzzled by the unexpected kindness he had received from the bartender, for past experience had led him to suspect unsolicited help.

As he rode, his clear, cold brain tried to fit the unexpected events of that day to the happenings which in such a short time had reduced him from being an up-and-coming cattleman to a jailbird, a man who many said had been lucky to escape the rope, a man who had been convicted of murdering his foreman. And if it hadn't been for the clever attorney who, despite his client's instructions, had insisted on bringing into the open that unsavoury business of his wife, Storm would have hung.

He forced himself to remember Alin's bitter, vengeful face when she had given her evidence; she had been so bitter that even though she'd denied having anything to do with Denton she had overcalled her hand and turned the jury at least part way in Rawhide's favour. Storm himself hadn't the least idea that there had been anything between Alin and Denton, not — that is — until a week before Denton had been found shot in the back in Thorn Coulee. Rawhide had ridden into Hawksbee that day to see about a couple of cattle cars for a small shipment of three-year-olds he had been going to make to El Paso; that business arranged, he'd gone into the *Last Stand* saloon for a couple of drinks; it had been late and the citizens of Hawksbee had been celebrating another day, but as Storm strode in the talk had stopped suddenly and was resumed only after an obvious pause. It had been as the talk picked up again he had heard the drunken, slurred words that had first aroused his suspicions, suspicions which had grown until crystalised by a note he'd found advising him to go to Thorn Coulee and watch.

Perhaps stupidly, he had gone, stupidly because he had realised he and Alin had been all washed up for a long time; he went because he would never enjoy being made a fool of — and then he had found Denton dead. Storm had taken him into El Paso and, to his utter amazement, had been arrested for murdering his foreman.

"Yeah," he muttered, as he touched spurs to the claybank and jerked the horse into a swinging lope — "yeah, some'un shore had that sewn up tight. Alin? Hell! I tried to figger that way thousan's o' times, but I'm still dang shore she never had th' brains. Then who'n hell else? I never been a popular cuss, but danged if I kin think o' anyone that didn't like me bad enough to frame me for murder."

He slowly built a cigarette, touched a match to it, then cursed himself for a fool. "Some'un framed me," he said, "an' I shore aim to find out who — an' to make him plumb sorry he done it. But whoever it was Alin was in it too — she shore had her story pat. Git along, hawse, we got quite a ways to travel an' maybe some'un tailin' us, though I don' figger either Lacy or Joe is gonna do much travellin' today. I wish some o' them other poor buzzards in th' pen could ha' seen them two roughin' each other up — shore would ha' made their day for 'em."

2

THE Rawhide who, a week later, rode into Hawksbee was, to all outward appearance, the same reserved, competent rider he had been before his trial and sentence; in reality he was a far more dangerous character. A hard, bitter man forged in the brutal fires of the 'pen', possessed by the fixed purpose of revenge. Seven days' riding had fined him down again and sweated off the 'pen' fat borne of too much starchy food. Sid the barman had given him a sack of the bare necessities, for the rest he'd got by on the sun-dried flesh of a buck he had killed; the first day's saddle soreness had gone and hours of practice each evening had regained him his skill with his Colts.

Dusk was falling on the wide, dusty main street of Hawksbee as the tired claybank's hoofs struck hollowly on the plank causeway into Seth Parker's livery stable. Seth, as usual at that time of evening, was not there, so Rawhide unsaddled his horse, rubbed him down and forked down a trough full of sweet-smelling hay before leaving him in a stall. Easing the saddle soreness out of his legs, he walked out and across the street to Ed Bond's little office.

He felt strange walking once again past the buildings he knew so well, strange and more bitter than ever, for those buildings had housed men he had thought were his friends, men with whom he had drunk, played poker, gossiped, men he'd met at barbecues, men with whom he'd done business, men who'd cheated him mildly, men who had smiled and slapped him on the back when he'd beaten them in a trade, men, who'd with hardly an exception, had turned against him when he had been on trial for his life. And now, strangely enough, he didn't hate them. He hadn't any feelings at all about them, not even about those who had been on the jury that had convicted him on evidence that had been partly circumstantial; he just didn't want to see them, wanted never to see them again. He had come to Hawksbee for one purpose and one purpose only — to pick up the months' cold trail of the man who had fixed it for him to hang for Denton's killing.

As Storm strode through the dust of the street he saw several men he knew; knew, too, that they saw him, a sneer quirking on his lips as each in his own fashion discovered urgent business in the opposite direction. With the sneer still on his lips Storm pushed open the lopsided door of the sheriff's office, the sagging board floor creaking under his feet as he entered.

"Figgered you'd be in days ago," Sheriff Ed Bond said from the gloom at the back of the office where Rawhide knew the law officer spent many hours seeing how far down in his chair the base of his spine would go. Now he lurched up and gripped hands with his one-time prisoner, said curtly, "Glad to see you, Rawhide. Should I light th' lamp?"

"Guess not, Ed. Some'un in this town wanted me dead pretty bad; maybe they still do, an' I reckon th' county ain't got around to buyin' you no curtains yet."

"They ain't, But they still pay me enough for whisky."

Rawhide heard a drawer scrape open, then the clink of a bottle against glass.

"Have a chair, Rawhide," the sheriff said, "an' drink hearty."

Storm felt his way to a chair, tipped it back against the wall where he could watch both window and door, then reached for the glass Bond pushed across the desk.

"Bad in th' 'pen?'" Bond queried impersonally.

"Yeah — funny thing, they seemed to have it in for me, couldn't do nothin' right. It ain't no bed o' roses, them jailers is plenty rough an' there ain't no questions asked when a prisoner gits killed."

"You reckon they was out to kill you?"

Rawhide shrugged. "Can't be shore," he replied, "but it looked thataway. Reckon I was lucky to git out."

"Yeah. Guess I better tell you why I wrote that letter."

Rawhide grinned as he lifted his glass to his lips. "Nice o' you, Ed. I shore as hell know you hate writin' like poison."

"Never did git beyond second grade, still I hadda do somethin' when that greaser come in to see me."

Rawhide said, "What greaser?"

"Miguel Patoulos. Know him?"

"Yeah — kinda. Was him got in trouble down Goldhawk way, huh?"

"That's th' jasper. Seems you know him some."

"A little. Miguel ain't a bad greaser, an' he had a wife an' 'bout seventeen kids."

Bond grunted. "His fault," he growled. "All these spicks are the same — any one o' them'd steal th' gold outa yore teeth, an' seems like that was what Miguel was doin' that day when Denton got shot."

"Rustlin'?"

"Wa'al, hardly. I'd say it was small time stuff, jus' beefin' a steer likely. Anyway, whatever he was doin', he was doin' it overlookin' th' bluff above Thorn Coulee. He seen Denton an' laid low, figgerin' Denton was trailin' him; he seen th' murderer but couldn't recognise him, but he was plumb certain it wasn't you."

"But why in hell didn't he come forward at th' trial?"

"Seems he hadda go south, likely to run some rustled cows across th' border, then he got in trouble in Benedaro an' got tossed in jail for a couple o' months. He'd on'y jus' made it back an' didn't even know you'd been charged with murder."

"Uhuh. Jus' my bad luck."

"Yeh." Bond cleared his throat nervously.

"An' you ain't got no idea who done th' killin'?"

"Not any. Y'see, Rawhide, when I had you in th' hoosegow I kinda didn't think to look no further."

"An' now th' trail's six months cold."

"It is. Ain't so funny. Me, I ain't long in brains, I never figgered this detective stuff not none at all; gimme a snarled trail to follow an' I'm awright. But, well, Rawhide, I jus' ain't got no ideas about this set-up." He coughed again and felt for and refilled the glasses.

Rawhide knew the sheriff had some more news to give him — and unpleasant news at that.

"What you figger to do, Rawhide?" Bond went on, with as near an approach to nervousness as was possible. "Goin' to carry on th' ranch?"

"Could be. Why?"

"Take another drink, feller. I — I

guess I gotta tell you — you ain't got no spread no more."

Rawhide's chair crashed forward on the floor. "What'n hell you mean, Ed? No spread! I had close on four thousan' head!"

"Not any more you ain't, Rawhide. Yore wife done sold 'em!"

"Alin? But, hell, Ed, she couldn't ha' done! They weren't hers! She couldn't give title for 'em! I kin claim 'em back!"

"You couldn't, not even if you could find 'em. Th' law says a man's gotta support his wife, an' you bein' in jail Alin figgered she'd jus' haveta do th' best she could for herself."

"She shore did," Rawhile breathed. "She shore did. That herd — why, I spent years buildin' it up. She — she — why, she musta got close on a hundred thousan' bucks!"

"Not as much as that — none o' the ranchers round here would buy from her an' she hadda git a dealer out from Montgomery."

"What happens to th' range?" Rawhide couldn't see Bond, but he knew the sheriff's shoulders lifted in a slow shrug.

"You know th' way it is, Rawhide — leased range, an' soon's some'un quits usin' it th' other fellers start easin' over on to it. Box T had some; Lary Y headed in at th' water hole on Elk Flats."

Rawhide cursed savagely. "That Yates," he muttered. "Bastard's been after that water hole for years — an' now he's got it. I s'pose she didn't git to take th' ranch-house with her as well, huh?"

"Wa'al, no, not quite, but she sold every dang thing in it, horses, wagons, buckboard, tools, stocks, everythin'. Rawhide, she shore acted th' way she didn't expect you'd ever come back. I guess she didn't write you?"

"Not any — not that I'd ha' got it, I never got no letters at all. Where at is she now, Ed?"

"Dunno — quite; she pulled out on

th' Westbound maybe three — four weeks ago; she'd fixed all yore punchers afore she left."

"All of 'em? Hell, Ed, some o' those boys had been with me for years!"

"I know — all 'cept one she fired, she jus' kept one on for a spell to help around th' place, that was after all th' stock had gone an' while she was waitin' for a reservation. Funny, I don' remember seein' that feller around th' town after she left; th' rest o' th' boys stayed for a spell, looked like they were kinda lost."

"Guess they would be; jobs are scarce. So all I got left is th' land th' ranch-house is on — that's homesteaded."

"Yeah, she couldn't sell that. There was a feller out to look at it th' other day, Eastern jasper, reppin' for a cattle company, I figgered, plumb close-mouthed an' wouldn't say how he come to hear of it."

"He still in town?"

"Think so. Say, Rawhide, I — I feel

purty bad tellin' you all this."

"It ain't good, Ed, but I guess I'll jus' havta add it t' th' score I got awready. Kinda queer her takin' a puncher with her. 'Member who it was?"

"Dunno. I didn't pay no particular attention. Y'see, folks kinda moved out o' th' way when she come by on account o' she . . . "

"Yeah, Ed, I know. Know where she went?"

"Station agent would, he made her th' reservation."

"Guess I'll see him in th 'mornin'. Right now, Ed, I figger to try an' find this Eastern jasper. I'm flat busted an' I'll take what I kin git for th' ranch — if I sell it to a company they'll dang soon grab back th' range I leased an' then Yates kin whistle for his water hole. Where at's this feller stayin'?"

"Bates Hotel. I'll come with you, Rawhide, I guess maybe you'll need a witness to say you're th' owner o' th' Circle S. Lemme grab my hat an' I'll be right with you!" The sheriff's chair creaked as he heaved his bulk up and out of it, the floor groaned as he moved across to the door. "Gettin' kinda hard to find a cayuse that kin carry me," he admitted as he pulled the door open and edged his prominent belly through the entrance — "an' I'm too dang big a target too!"

Rawhide followed him, eyes automatically alert for trouble with that constant watchfulness which becomes habitual to a man who lives dangerously — if he wants to go on living; now, not for the first time, Storm's caution saved his life. As he moved from the door of the sheriff's office on to the sagging boardwalk he saw light glint along the length of a rifle barrel which emerged from the shadows beside the livery stable; he moved on the instant, shoving the portly sheriff asprawl in the thick dust of the street, the recoil of his thrust helping his own dive to the left for the shelter of a porch post. Across the street, flame jetted with the whiplash crack of a Winchester. Rawhide heard the bullet splinter its way through the sun-warped boards of the sheriff's office and then the explosion of his own Colt jarred the heel of his right hand.

"What'n Tophet?" Bond spluttered, rolling over in the dust like a shrouded porpoise.

"Keep down, Ed!" Rawhide urged. "That feller kin shoot." His own Colt roared again as he spoke, and he was rewarded by a grunt from the other side of the street; the rifle clanged again, but Rawhide could tell from the muzzle flash that the aim was way off.

"You got him, Rawhide?" the sheriff bawled as he dragged out his own gun and blazed away. After the last shot Rawhide heard a pile of empty cans clatter down.

"C'mon, he's gettin' away!" He crossed the street at a run, dived up the alley beside the livery stable and through to the garbage littered space behind just in time to see his quarry reaching the thick brush which grew beyond the waste space; almost of its own volition his gun went off, the man staggered and lurched — then crumpled, his head actually falling amongst the bushes which would have spelt safety to him.

"Who'n hell is he?" Bond gasped, his breath jerky by running.

Rawhide struck a match, rolled the body over to illuminate the face on which death had frozen a look of surprise. "Stranger to me," he said.

"Me too," the sheriff gasped. "I ain't even seen him around town. Turn out his pockets, Rawhide, maybe that'll tell us somethin'. Was it you or me he was after?"

"Me," Rawhide replied curtly. "He could ha' shot you twenty times while you was easin' yore belly through that door. Reckon th' county had oughta give you a wider door, Ed."

"Be all from you, feller. Where'n hell is my dang deppity, he ain't never around when . . . Aargh! Here you are, Al — late as usual. Know this jasper?"

The deputy had brought a lantern with him, and Rawhide stood back while the two law officers examined the would-be murderer.

"Name's Willis," Bond said, "an' apart from that — nothin'. Cash, tobacco, matches — that's all. No dice. You seen him around, Al? No? Awright, git Doc to take th' body, county'll have to bury th' buzzard. C'mon, Rawhide, let's go see this Eastern feller if he ain't lef' town; name's Meek, but he shore don' look it."

★ ★ ★

"That's him — end o' th' bar."

Bates Hotel bar was pretty crowded, but the man whom Bond had indicated to Rawhide had quite a clear space round him at his end of the bar. He stood with one heel hooked in the brass rail and an expression on his face as if someone had just broken a

31

rotten egg under his nose; as Storm turned away from looking at him a voice bawled, "Hi, Rawhide! So they finally hammered some sense into Ed's thick head an' let you out, huh? Shake, ol' timer!"

Rawhide stared frostily into Bate's bloodshot eyes and didn't see the proffered hand.

"Hi, Bates," he said disinterestedly. "You drinkin', Ed?"

"Yeah, bourbon," the sheriff replied, smothering a chuckle at the hotel keeper's discomfiture; Bates had been on the jury at Storm's trial, had all along shown his conviction that Storm was guilty; now he turned away, his face flushed a mottled red, and a barkeep set out the drinks. Rawhide sipped his, nodded to Bond, then eased along the bar to the man Meek, who half-turned towards him.

"I hear you been sniffin' round th' Circle S," Rawhide said, not bothering to make his voice in the least friendly.

Meek looked at him as if the smell

under his nose had got worse.

"It's a free country, ain't it?"

"Shore. But it happens I like to know when an' why folks look over my property."

Meek's expression changed, became slightly less suspicious.

"You're Storm? But I thought . . ."

"I was in jail. Shore — I was, but I ain't now."

"But I don' understand . . ."

"They let me out. Ask th' sheriff if you don' believe me — he's right there. Why was you out at th' Circle S?"

"Heard it was for sale."

"That so?"

"You aimin' to buy?"

"Could be. You sellin'?"

"At a price. But I'd admire to know how you heard it was for sale."

"Don' see that matters to you."

"No? Wa'al, it does. An' I figger ten thousan' bucks."

"Forgit that, Storm. Cross a zero offa that figger!"

"Thousan' bucks for my spread? You

nuts? Why, it's got good water, feed, an' th' buildings alone . . . "

"Yeah, maybe a thousan' is low. Say five, huh?"

"Seven. That's a lucky number."

"Five's th' limit, Storm. I ain't buyin' for me. An' you gotta remember th' property's rundown some an' I'll guess we'll have trouble gettin' th' water."

"Awright, five. But I gotta know how you heard it was for sale."

"I ain't sayin' — but if I tell you we had a letter from Mountain City . . . "

"Arizona, huh?"

"Yeah."

"When did it come?"

"Two — three weeks ago."

"Thanks, Meek. There ain't but one lawsharp in town; meet me there at ten tomorrow."

Meek nodded, they gripped hands briefly and then the buyer returned to his expression of aloof superciliousness as Rawhide turned away.

"Done business?" the sheriff queried.

"Yeah. I sold th' spread."

"What you aimin' to do, feller?"

"What you think, Ed?"

"Goin' after her? Yeah, I figgered that."

"I'll be lookin' for th' man too, Ed."

The sheriff looked puzzled.

"What man?" he asked.

"Must ha' been a man, Ed. Whoever framed me for that murder had brains, an' Alin ain't long on brains, so I figger it musta been one o' my own punchers — some'un who knew what was goin' on around th' ranch, an' it could be that Denton had found out about him an' Alin. Now I come to think of it I seem to remember that Denton had been actin' kinda strange for a couple o' days — like he had somethin' on his mind an' didn't know whether to tell me or not."

"What about her?"

"Alin? We hadn't been speakin' much, it was comin' up for round-up an' I was busy . . . say, ain't that

35

Elmer over there? Th' depot agent? Hey, Elmer!"

The railroad man pushed his way through the crowd.

"Hiya, Rawhide! Heard you was back. How's tricks, ol' timer?" They shook hands, and Rawhide couldn't help but feel pleased at the pleasure in the agent's eyes.

"I'm pullin' outa Hawksbee, Elmer."

"Don' blame you. Goin' west?"

"Yeah. Say, Elmer, you 'member Alin goin'?"

"Shore. She wanted a reservation to Denver, took me plenty o' trouble to fix it."

"'Member th' feller as went with her?"

"I 'member there was one puncher she took, said he was gonna help her with her dunnage, feller called — called . . . Hell, Rawhide, I fergit. He was a big feller, blond, would be around a hundred an' eighty pounds — twenty-four or five I'd guess, kind of a neat dresser."

"Saxby?"

"Yeah, Saxby, that's th' one. Hadn't been with you long. I figgered it was queer she didn't pick Jenks or Wilkis, or one o' th' other ones that had been with you for years, 'stead of a Johnny-come-lately."

3

"**M**OUNTAIN CITY? It ain't much of a place, main street's purty steep, runs up a sorta canyon, trees back o' th' buildings each side; was a minin' camp till th' silver played out, some ranchin' around."

Rawhide, his body giving easily to the lurchings and swayings of the old coach in which he was travelling from Enderby, hardly heard what the driver was telling him in answer to his questions; he hadn't hurried his journey from Hawksbee, and during the weeks he had spent on the trail he'd let his beard grow so that he was pretty confident even his wife wouldn't know him; he hadn't thought much either about her or about Saxby, in fact he hadn't thought much at all, doing his travelling in a curiously detached way as if watching the man Storm methodically pursuing what he then thought was the sole object of his life — revenge. He realised that once that object was attained he would go on living, but until he and Saxby had faced each other over drawn guns, what would happen afterwards didn't enter into his calculations.

The stage lurched wildly as the trail pitched downwards to a dry wash, the driver cracked his whip beside the leader's ear and swore picturesquely at his six horses as they settled against their collars to drag the heavy coach up the steep, winding slope beyond the wash, he cursed even more luridly as, on rounding a rocky bend, he found the trail completely blocked by a long Conestoga wagon that sagged drunkenly on the splayed spokes on a broken off-side rear wheel. As the driver slammed on his brake a thin-faced, haggard-looking man rose from his knees beside the wheel and stared helplessly up at the fuming driver.

"Git outa my goddam way!" the

driver bawled. "I gotta schedule to fill!"

The man's shoulders lifted dismally. "I'm sorry. Our wheel broke an' I . . . " His voice trailed away as his hands twisted uselessly.

"Dang th' luck," the driver grumbled. "All th' places along th' trail these dang settlers could use t' break down he hasta pick this 'un!"

Rawhide swung down from his seat beside the driver and walked towards the wagon. Close to, he could see that both man and outfit had known better days; the man wore patched and ragged store clothes, the canvas tilt of the wagon was threadbare in places, its warped boards hung with household goods.

"Goin' far?" he asked the man, his eyes busy with the evidence of near poverty.

"Californy," the man replied, eyes brightening a little at the hint of sympathy in Rawhide's attention. "We're from Ohio; th' wife's sick an' I figgered

— I — I had a store, sold up an' come west."

"Dad, I can't hold these horses much longer!" A clear, firm voice, a girl's voice, but one which held a note of determination. Rawhide eased past the wagon to where he could see the four scrubby horses and the tall, dark-haired girl who was doing more harm than good by trying to hold them.

"Easy on them reins, miss," Rawhide advised.

"Who are you?" the girl demanded.

"Name's Storm," he told her, abruptly aware that he liked the direct gaze of her clear, grey eyes and the curves of her firm mouth. "It ain't no use keepin' 'em harnessed until we got th' wheel mended."

"Mended?" she queried bitterly. "Even if you do get it mended something else will break."

"Now, Marcia, it ain't all that bad," her father protested weakly. "If this gentleman . . . "

Rawhide undid the harness, led the

41

horses out of the pole shaft and up the trail to a patch of bunch grass where they started placidly to graze; as he went back he saw the girl's eyes fasten upon the two low-slung Colts he wore.

"We'll have no help from a gunman," she said coldly.

"Don' be a fool," he retorted equally coldly. "You're blockin' th' trail."

"You really mustn't say such things, Marcia! If this gentleman is kind enough . . . " the man's voice trailed away again. It appeared he had difficulty in finishing any statement he might try to make.

Storm shrugged, went round to the back of the wagon and knelt to look at the wheel; as he did so a voice from inside the tilt asked:

"David, what's happening? Are we broken down again?"

"My wife, she . . . It's all right, dear. We — we have a little trouble, but . . . "

"Got any rawhide?" Storm asked.

42

Three spokes had broken and two were cracked; the broken spokes had come out of their sockets in hub and rim.

"Why, yes, I think so. I — we saved the skin of a steer we killed a while back." The man climbed in through the tilt and Storm heard some low-voiced talk; then he turned to see the girl — Marcia — watching him.

"I suppose you think we're fools?" she said.

Rawhide rolled a cigarette, touched a match to it and looked round him before he said, "No, there ain't no man a fool for doin' what he figgers is best. Been kind of a hard trip, huh?"

"It hasn't been easy," she admitted; his words seemed to have released some kind of tension. "We — well, we're tenderfeet really. We — we don't seem to learn much. Pa had most of our money stolen in Denver; we'd been all right until then."

The man climbed down out of the wagon, dragging a cowhide which was stiff as a board, and dry.

"Haveta soak it," Storm said. "Git a bucket o' water. Hey, Mac! C'mon an' gimme a hand if you wanta git to Mountain City today!"

Grumbling, the coach driver clambered down from his box and cursed under his breath as Storm made him get the coach's unditching bar out; together they levered up the wagon's axle, wedged it with stones and freed the broken wheel. Storm laid the wheel out, straightened the spokes, pushed them back in their sockets, and then, with strips of soaked rawhide he bound them in place.

"But surely that won't hold?" Marcia queried.

The coach-driver chuckled. "Hold stronger'n a vice," he told her. "Rawhide shrinks when it dries — ten minutes in this sun an' that wheel'll be as good as new — maybe better!" In the fierce heat the rawhide dried quickly, contracting so powerfully that the wood of the wheel cracked as it was clamped into place; Storm eased it back on

44

the axle, then hammered home the lynch-pin.

"Ready for off now," he said.

"I — I really don't know how to thank you. I — I'm David Foran — and I — I . . . "

"Ain't no need for thanks," Storm told him. "Hitch up yore cayuses an' git movin'. So long, Miss!" He touched a hand to his hat and turned away to the coach where the driver already sat on his box.

"Maybe they'll be awright now for a spell," the driver grumbled as Rawhide sat down beside him. "Them Easterners!"

"Many along this trail?"

"Quite some; Mountain City's just 'bout th' las' place afore they cross th' Journada."

"Journada?"

"Yeah. Journada del Meurte, one malo piece o' country over to Palo Seco in Californy. Me, I wouldn't cross it for a million bucks; some of 'em git through."

"Only some?"

"Yeah. There ain't much water an' what there is is mos'ly alkali. Still, if they do git across it they saves 'bout a thousan' miles; lot of 'em take one look an' turn back, guess that's what these Forans'll do."

Rawhide rubbed his chin; that girl, for all she was inexperienced, wasn't one to give up easily, he reckoned she'd go on until the end.

"Yeah," he said slowly, "feller didn't seem to have much git-up-an'-git."

In front of them, Foran had at last got his horses harnessed after making pretty heavy weather of it; the girl looked back at the coach, shading her eyes with her hand; she gave a tiny wave that might almost not have been a wave then she climbed up in front of the wagon as it lurched slowly into movement up the slope.

"Naw, he ain't much use," the driver agreed as he slapped the reins on his horses' rumps. "It's th' wimmen that cause th' trouble. Sick wife he had, but I'll bet it was her made him quit store-keepin' an' go to pioneerin' where he ain't got a cat's chance in hell."

"He said he reckoned Californy would cure her."

"Maybe it would, on'y she won't ever git there. Th' Journada'll see to that." He grunted, swung his leaders wide and sent the coach lurching past the lumbering wagon; Foran didn't look up, he was too busy handling his team. Marcia Foran's eyes settled briefly at the coach and away from Rawhide's as swiftly; for some reason he felt the blood mount in his cheeks, maybe because he was annoyed she hadn't waved to him again, and then he was unaccountably annoyed with himself because he'd even given it a thought.

From the dry wash the trail wound pretty steadily up the slopes of Green Mountain. The six coach horses didn't have an easy time of it and Rawhide found he couldn't help thinking about the laden, rickety wagon which the four near-foundered horses were trying to drag up behind him; then he pushed the thought out of his mind by asking the driver questions about the Journada del Meurte, and forcing himself to concentrate on the man's rambling replies. No, the driver hadn't crossed it himself but he knew people who had — both ways, though it was apparently worse if one was travelling westwards rather than eastwards, quite why, the driver couldn't tell, but every man who had crossed both ways said the same thing.

It became crystal clear to Rawhide that the Journada was no crossing to be undertaken by a party of tender-feet so indifferently equipped as the Forans; then he mentally shrugged his shoulders. "It ain't none o' my business," he told himself. "Man does what he figgers is best for his folks, an' as for wimmen — they're pizen!" He must have spoken the last statement out loud, for it set the driver off on a long, rambling story about some dance-hall girl who had taken him for his roll many years before; the loss still rankled.

In two hours they had left the cottonwood and live oak behind, were above the sumacs and cypresses and among the jack-pines; these, in turn, thinned, and the driver at last pulled up to breathe his horses for the fourth or fifth time on the scrub-covered crest of Green Mountain.

"There's th' Journada," he said, pointing westward, and Rawhide looked out and down upon more country than he'd ever seen before. In the clear desert air he could see for miles a huge expanse of sand and cactus merging into the purple distance.

"Sand an' snakes an' bad water," the driver said bitterly. "Close to four hundred miles an' no proper water — grass that ain't grass an' trees that ain't trees, an' a sun that sucks th' marrow outa yore bones."

"Any Injuns?"

"Used to be — not many years back; ain't now less'n they've busted offa th' reservation. Giddup, broncs! Ain't so long now."

They drove on down the trail, blinking in the nearly level rays of the sun setting far to the westward behind the rampart of mountains which marked the end of the Journada, the last murderous climb that barred the traveller from the 'Promised Land' of California.

Dusk was falling as the driver released his brake a little, let the heavy old stage go creaking and lurching through the dust and rocks of Mountain City's main street to pull it up with his usual flourish outside the express office.

"Mountain City — end o' th' line! All change!" he bawled, rather unnecessarily, since Rawhide was the only passenger. "Dowd's Hotel ain't so bad," he advised. "It's th' on'y one in town."

Rawhide nodded, "So long, an' thanks!" He shouldered his bedroll and climbed down to allow the stage to go on under the arch of the livery stable; then he turned to face a little crowd of idlers, his eyes passing swiftly from face to face. Saxby wasn't among them. He straightened his shoulders, eased the fingers of his right hand which had unconsciously tensed and realised that, now it had come to the point, he couldn't be any too sure of recognising the man he intended to kill. A tall, thick-set man lounged forward; he wore a battered star and a drooping, tobacco-stained moustache.

"Lookin' for some'un?" he queried.

"What makes you think I am?"

"Marshal Wiley; I aim to keep th' law here, it's my business to notice things. You looked us over right close an' was all set to pull a gun."

Rawhide smiled thinly. "Guess maybe I was," he admitted. "Where's a good place to take th' dust outa our throats?"

Wiley smiled back. "Best is nearest," he replied, and led the way into the Placer — a biggish place, well furnished with gambling layouts and an air of quiet. Rawhide slid quickly through the door and off to one side, alert, watchful; there were only about half a dozen men in the house, one rolling craps by himself, four playing blackjack, and the sixth — the barman — watching the game, leaning on one elbow on the bar. He straightened up as Wiley crossed to the long bar.

"What'll it be, Marshal?"

"Bourbon. An' for you, friend?"

"Th' same — an' on me," Rawhide said, flipping a double eagle on the bar as the glasses spun along. "Leave th' bottle," he said, "an' pour one for yoreself."

The marshal filled his glass and emptied it with a quick, practised flip of his wrist. "Luck!" he said curtly. "Dry travellin'?"

"Stage was late — wagon stalled comin' up outa a dry wash."

"Uhuh. More for Californy?"

"Yeah — an' plumb helpless."

"Friend, they all are. Th' trouble they are t' me!" he sighed, filled and emptied his glass again then looked at it as if mildly surprised at his own action; just in case he'd been mistaken he repeated the action. "Yeah, dang nuisance," he said, "always bleatin' an' sayin' they been robbed. Maybe they have, but they shore as hell ask for it. This feller you're lookin' for — would he be a settler?"

"Not any. Puncher of 'bout twenty-six or seven, would be around a hundred an' eighty pounds, six foot, blond."

"Hundreds o' them around here."

"He would ha' got here 'bout four or five weeks ago."

"They come an' go all th' time. He got a name?"

"Had one — Saxby. But he would ha' changed it, I guess."

"Uhuh. You law?"

"Private."

"Awright, I ain't pryin'. He done you dirt?"

"An' then some."

"Too bad. I'll ask around, but — wa'al,

you know how it is!"

Rawhide nodded, refilled his own glass; he knew just how it was, but he couldn't be sure whether or not Wiley was telling the truth. Maybe he didn't know Saxby, but again, maybe he did and had been 'squared.' After all, if Saxby had access to all the cash Alin had obtained for the Circle S cattle he had plenty to persuade a small-town marshal to keep his mouth shut. He pushed the bottle over to the barman.

"Take a drink, Mack," he said. "You heard my spiel to th' marshal. It mean anythin' to you?"

Just the merest flicker passed between the marshal and the barman before the latter shook his head.

"Like the marshal said, there's hundreds would add up to that. Sorry."

Suddenly there was an atmosphere of tension, suspicion in the saloon. Even the blackjack players felt it and looked round from their game.

"What makes you so shore he's

here?" Wiley queried. "You trailed him?"

Rawhide shrugged. "Ain't shore — I got reasons." Some pride deep within him prevented him from asking any questions about Alin.

"Guess I'll be ramblin'," he said. "I need a room an' some chuck. Where at is Dowd's Hotel?"

"Up street a piece, 'bout three blocks."

"Chuck there?"

"Not any. One block further — Chink restaurant. Food's good."

"Thanks, Wiley. So long!" Storm shouldered his bedroll and went out; neither the marshal nor the barman said anything about the half-empty bottle. Outside, Rawhide tramped heavily along the boardwalk, then stepped quietly off into the dust of the alley beside the Placer. Only minutes later the marshal emerged and looked up and down the street quickly, then he set off down at a fast walk; Rawhide dumped his bedroll, followed, keeping to the shadows as the law officer went on until all the saloons and stores were past. He then turned aside to a rough tumbledown shack and pounded on the door which opened to reveal a thin strip of lamplight.

"Reckon he's here," Rawhide heard the marshal say, then the door shut again and the law officer started back.

Rawhide smiled thinly, flattened into a doorway and watched Wiley back to the Placer. He then picked up his bedroll and went on towards Dowd's Hotel. It was rough, but the room he was given looked fairly clean; he dumped his roll, had a wash, then went on up the street and ate a meal at the Chink's place. After his meal he sat over his fourth cup of bitter coffee trying to decide what to do next, trying to imagine what Saxby would do.

In Saxby's place Rawhide would have been eager for them to meet, but from what he remembered of the puncher he didn't think that would be Saxby's reaction. Saxby had, he thought, been a quiet, rather self-effacing man who had been clever at avoiding the dirtiest riding jobs; he was never there when a water-hole had to be cleaned out, or some extra branding had to be done away from the branding chutes; it was curious, Rawhide thought, how little he really remembered about Saxby, which made it all the more difficult to forecast what the fellow would do.

Not for one moment did he doubt that Alin and Saxby were in Mountain City, or that Saxby had paid Wiley to watch for all incoming travellers; Saxby would know by this time that he was in town, and Rawhide's mouth tightened at the thought, a tingle of excitement ran up his spine at the realisation that at that moment Saxby might be across street from the Chink's place, eyes squinting along the sights of a rifle; he had arranged for a man to be ready in Hawksbee; in Mountain City he would be ready himself.

Rawhide got to his feet, stretched and flexed his muscles, and checked his guns.

"You got a back door?" he asked the Chinaman when he paid his check.

The Oriental nodded and led the way silently through a chaotic kitchen where he pointed to a door. Rawhide saw the dirty, uncurtained windows staring out at the darkness; he reached up and turned out the lamp before he opened the door, standing aside from the opening before bending out into the darkness. A wind stirred the trees which clothed the steep slope of the gulch behind the restaurant and the rising moon peopled the shadows with hidden riflemen, but no shot blazed from the darkness, and Rawhide got back to Dowd's Hotel with no more difficulty than that imposed by the rough ground. He could find no back door, so eased carefully round to the front porch; moonlight shone on to one end of the wide, sagging porch — the nearer side; the open front door was invitingly near, but so strong was his sense of danger that he went back round the building, swung himself

58

quietly over the porch rail and moved along past the windows and in through the door. A lamp burned dimly in the hall, and the hotel owner — or at least the man who had taken Rawhide's money — slept noisily in a rocking chair by the stairs. For some minutes Rawhide stood watching the man, his hands crooked over his guns, for it appeared to him that the snores were not quite regular enough to be genuine; there was something false about them. Then he saw that Dowd — if that was his name — appeared to slumber with the uncomfortable bulk of a Colt sticking hard into one of his fat hams.

Rawhide crossed the hall swiftly, drew a Colt and prodded Dowd's belly under his folded hands; Dowd gasped, groaned, opened his small eyes, and swore.

"What'n hell's th' idea? Can't a man have his sleep? Jus' cause you room here don' give you th' right."

"Anyone been askin' for me?"

The small, cunning eyes went blank.

"Why should they? You Leonidas Polk hidin' behind that beard?"

"Leave th' clever stuff. Wiley been here?"

"No. An' why should th' law want you?"

"It don't. Git up!"

"Why?"

Rawhide gave him another prod with the Colt muzzle.

"You're gonna take a walk — up to my room."

"I ain't. I like it here."

Rawhide sighed. "Look, Dowd," he said, "I ain't a patient man an' I ain't shot a hotel keeper in quite a while; I wouldn't want to start over. Git up an' git walkin'." He pulled back the hammer of a Colt; the click was loud in the silence. Dowd's face paled.

"I — I — you got me wrong. I — I never . . ."

"Maybe, but I don' aim to take no chances. Up!"

Ponderously, Dowd heaved his flacid bulk up out of the chair and started to climb the stairs which creaked under his weight.

"I dunno what you figger's happened," he grumbled loudly. "I awready took you up to yore room once. I don' aim to have no trouble in my place."

Along the landing above, a door closed, and Rawhide, a gun held in Dowd's back, nodded once; he made Dowd precede him to his room, then — his eyes shuttling between the three other doors — he said, "Open it up." Keeping the hotel keeper's bulk between him and those other doors which might open sufficiently for a gun muzzle to be pushed through the crack.

Dowd leant his bulk on the door which swung right back; moonlight streamed through the uncurtained window and showed the bare room to be empty.

"There, no trouble, huh?"

"Not th' way I played it," Rawhide replied, easing into the room. "Beat it!"

Grumbling, Dowd lumbered back towards the stairs as Rawhide closed the door, whipping away from it as he did so; nothing happened, nothing at all, no shot, no sound but the creak of the stairs as Dowd went down, and the mournful call of a nightjar from the trees behind the hotel.

"But I ain't a fool," Rawhide muttered. "I'm shore as hell Saxby was layin' for me. I jus' am shore as hell." He sat on the bed, out of line from the door, and stared at the pattern cast by the moonlight on the boards of the floor. "All th' chances are on his side," he went on, "th' dang skunk! He's gotten th' law on his side, an' that's so crooked it'd screw inta th' floor. Maybe I should ha' played it different — maybe I should. But, hell, too late now. Way I started I'll have to go on." And at that moment a fingernail scratched at the door.

"Who is it?" he asked.

"Alin! Let me in, Richard."

Rawhide laughed, a short, harsh bark of a laugh.

"Yeah? Jus' like that?"

"I gotta see you, talk with you. I jus' gotta!"

"What about? Them thousan's o' steers o' mine you sold? An' Saxby?"

"Yes — and other things. I — I was a good wife to you once. For Gawd's sake listen to me now. I'm alone — Saxby doesn't know."

Maybe I'm a fool, Rawhide told himself, but I believe her. "Awright," he said out loud. "C'mon in, an' be careful. I gotta gun on you!"

She slipped into the room at once, her manner as agitated and scared as her voice had been; for some seconds she leant against the closed door, listening, then she shivered and faced Rawhide. He saw she had become thinner, her blonde hair was dull and untidy, her face lined and her eyes anxious.

"You don' look like you're enjoyin' life," he commented.

"Richard, I did you dirt, ain't no use denyin' it, but I was goin' crazy at that ranch with no one to talk to, no clothes, no parties, an' you — you didn't care for nothin' but th' ranch."

"I was gettin' ahead — makin' money for you to spend."

"Yeah, maybe, but then Dean come along . . ."

"Saxby?"

"Yeah. Dean an' me, we liked each other first off; he tol' me about big cities, Denver an' Salt Lake an' New York. He said he'd been there an' how he'd like to take me. Denton caught us one day, said he'd give me three days to tell you. If I didn't he would. Dean saw at once how we could get rid of both o' you an' have plenty o' money to go to all those wonderful places."

"So you framed me, huh?"

"Yeah." She swallowed hard. "It ain't no use sayin' I'm sorry — but I am, Richard, real sorry."

"I'm alive — Denton ain't. Yore sorrow ain't much use to him, is it?"

"Ain't no use rubbin' it in; I've suffered."

"Yeah? Why?"

"Saxby." She almost hissed the name and her hands clenched into talons. "I'd like to scratch his guts out an' hang 'em on a cactus while he's still alive."

Rawhide smiled thinly.

"I thought you two was in love?"

"I did. I doubt if he was ever after anythin' but money. That's all he ever wants — money for drink, money for gamblin', money for other women. Yeah, that too. First off we went to Denver, then we were gonna buy a ranch with th' money I got for th' cattle . . ."

"Thought you didn't like livin' on a ranch?"

"I know, but Dean . . ."

"You mean you reckoned you could git along awright on a ranch with him but not with me, huh?"

"Well, yeah, I guess that must be so, but he never bought th' ranch. We

65

seen plenty, but he said they wouldn't do. He had a different reason every time, an' he was nearly always drunk; then he left Denver an' came west, through smaller an' smaller places until we landed here."

"Nice place you picked."

"Don' be like that, Richard — hard an' nasty. I know I . . ."

"Look here, Alin," he told her sharply, "you done me plenty dirt an' you know I ain't th' forgivin' sort. What you want with me?"

"You wouldn't take me back?"

"Danged right I wouldn't — not unless hell freezes over."

She looked down, her fingers kneading her far from clean dress.

"Then I guess — I guess I'll haveta kill myself," she whispered.

Rawhide shrugged. "It's a free country," he said indifferently. "What about Saxby?"

"That beast? He's struck me! Look!" She pulled up her skirt to show whip weals across one thigh.

"You picked him," Rawhide reminded her.

"He's a drunk, he's spent all th' money. He's even wrote to a cattle company tryin' to sell th' ranch."

"Too bad," Rawhide snapped. "Now git, Alin, an' don' come back. I don' mind you stealin' from me, I don' mind yore runnin' off with th' hired help, but I ain't standin' bein' framed for murder; as for takin' you back — no dice, Alin, so pull yore freight!"

"So you mean it — that you won't take me back?"

Rawhide just laughed — and then she cursed him, calling him every foul name to which she could lay her tongue. After that he felt better, for he had had an uneasy suspicion that if she'd pleaded with him he might have been weak enough to give her another chance. Once, he supposed, he had been in love with her, but that time had long since passed; for months, perhaps years, before Denton's murder he had been aware that her continual nagging complaints, her very presence, had become an increasing irritant to him, but only at that moment did he realise that her continued existence was a matter of complete indifference to him. She saw that in his eyes and cursed him again before storming out of his room. Once she'd gone Rawhide wedged the only chair under the door knob, spread his bedroll on the bed, pulled his boots off, unbuckled his guns and put one close to hand under the pillow, then he lay down and slept like the dead until long past dawn.

4

HE had breakfast at the Chink's place, then strolled back down street, toothpick between his teeth and eyes alert under his low-pulled hat; Mountain City evidently didn't believe in early rising, for there were few citizens about; one or two storekeepers lounged in the doors of their establishments, yawning and scratching themselves and occasionally relieving the monotony by spitting. Swampers were making a pretence of sweeping the dust and litter from saloon floors, inside the saloons barmen were polishing glasses, refilling spittoons. Rawhide walked slowly past noting everything, seeing nothing until he reached the shack to which Wiley had gone the previous evening. It was shut up — dead-looking; for some minutes he stood staring at it, wondering if

Saxby were inside.

"If he is, he won't be sobered up yet," he muttered to himself, "an' I should want him to know all about what's comin' to him. A clean death's too good for that sidewinder."

Rawhide turned and walked back a block or two to a barber's shop where a small, scrawny man welcomed him effusively.

"Shave, suh? Why, o' course! Always say if every man had him a beard us barbers'd never make us a livin'. Ha! Ha! Yeah, right over there. I'll jus' take it down with a taper, huh? Then razor th' rest." He set about his task busily and Rawhide watched in the cracked, fly-blown mirror while his growth of facial hair was whisked away; he was glad to see it go and rather annoyed that he had ever thought it would ever be any help.

"Stranger in town, huh?" the barber asked. "Come in on th' stage? Gittin' to be quite a place — Mountain City. Quite a place. Like our town? Figgerin' to settle? Ranchin's doin' good around, though th' miners ain't. Real estate? Wa'al, ain't so easy to find a place in town, gettin' to be a busy li'l burg. That shack down street, no, it ain't empty. Couple from Denver rent it from Tom Marsh, who's got th' hardware store; couple by th' name o' Smith. Him? Dunno quite, seems to be around town all th' time, drinks some an' gambles quite a piece. Yeah, blond feller an' would be about six foot; she's blonde, too, looks kinda scary an' don' talk to folks much. They don' git along too well, always scrappin'; don' blame her way he plays around — an' loses money. Yessir, th' boys shore have trimmed him for some since he hit town. He said he was gonna buy a ranch, but I reckon it'd be a flea ranch all he could buy now; he owes Tom Marsh for th' rent — an' still gambles. Ain't been home yet. Yeah, there was a big game goin' las' night — back room o' Marsh's store. Marsh he kin play poker some. He ain't got no wife an' he's had his back room fixed up real nice."

Rawhide guessed the barber did have a wife and did not have his back room 'fixed up real nice.'

"Th' game still goin' on?" he asked.

"Figger so. I ain't seen Lon Gates go home, an' Al Chamber's hawss is still tied up out front." He sighed and looked out of the door. "Nother o' them settlers wagons," he said. "Come through all th' time; lookit a map they do an' figger this is an easy way to Californy. It ain't!"

Rawhide looked out too and saw the Foran outfit pass slowly by. Foran himself trudged at the head of the lead horses. He looked tired, as did the girl who sat on the seat, a pale-looking woman beside her. Evidently they had pulled off the trail for the night and started on again at dawn.

The barber shook his head as he turned back to finish trimming Rawhide's hair. "Don' do th' town no good — them folks," he said.

"Why not? Brings in new people, don' it?"

"Maybe, but they ain't no use — most of 'em; ain't even got th' price of a shave, an' always yellin' they been gypped."

"An' have they?"

"Wa'al, you know how it is. Feller wants what you got, ain't but natural to up th' price a bit."

"An' mos'ly they ain't got th' cash?"

"Aw, some of 'em have it."

"An' those that don' have it have to go on across th' Journada th' way they are — without proper stores or equipment?"

The barber shrugged. "This town ain't a charity," he said, and all his previous tone of ingratiation had gone out of his voice, leaving it hard and metallic. Rawhide changed his ideas about the fellow.

"Naw, maybe it ain't, but there's a fair price — an' a price that's robbery, when a man needs it bad."

"They want stuff — they gotta pay."

"An' if they can't pay — let 'em die in th' desert?"

"They mos'ly would anyway. An', mister, I don' like yore tone. That'll be two bucks!"

Rawhide unwrapped the far from clean cloth from around his neck, stood up and wiped loose hairs from his face and neck.

"Feller," he said quietly, "you made a mistake — I ain't a settler an' I ain't gonna be gypped. A dollar is plenty!"

The barber faced him unmoved. "Two bucks," he repeated. "We got law in this town that . . . "

"That's tied in with all you nice kind traders, huh?" A gun appeared to leap into his hands. One instant it was in its holster, the next the muzzle jarred into the barber's stomach. "One buck is plenty, huh?" Rawhide said.

The barber backed until he fetched up against the wall. His hardness was only surface hardness — it had no depth. He was a small-time grifter trying to emulate the big boys in

Mountain City — and not getting by this time.

"Yeah, I — I guess maybe I made a mistake," he admitted in a voice half choked by fear. "One buck is all I earned!"

With his left hand Rawhide flipped a dollar on the littered floor and left the place while the barber was still scrabbling for the coin. As he walked away he saw that the Foran wagon had pulled up outside a store from inside which came a hoarse, jeering voice followed by a burst of laughter. Other men emerged from saloons and gambling joints and quite a crowd had collected by the time he reached the wagon.

"What gives?" he asked the girl Marcia who, one hand clenched round the brake, was gazing anxiously towards the open store door.

"Why — I — Oh, it's you? Dad — Dad went in and . . ."

There was another burst of laughter and more jeers from the raucous, drunken voice and, as Rawhide pushed his way inside, he heard the crashing reports of Colt shots. "Dance, you dang tenderfoot! Dance, dang you!"

Rawhide shoved through the crowd to see Foran clutching a pillar, his face ashen and the heels shot from his boots, facing — or trying to face — Saxby; Saxby, lurching with drunkenness, his face blotched and bloated with liquor, a still smoking Colt in each hand.

"Dance! Dance to hell an' gone!" Saxby bawled, and his Colts roared again, the bullets splintering the floor under Foran's feet. Drunk Saxby might be, but he could still shoot. Rawhide saw that, just as he saw that Foran — scared three parts to death though he was — had yet the mental courage to try to nerve his body to make a suicidal attempt to jump Saxby. Rawhide saw him tense himself, then he shoved through to the open space in the middle of the store.

"Jus' about all you're fit for — hazin'

pore saps that ain't got a gun!" he said quietly, in the silence that followed his sudden appearance.

Saxby stared, shook his head as if to try to clear his blurred vision; he closed one eye, then a shiver passed over his body. He flinched away and became aware that his hands still gripped his Colts, and that Rawhide hadn't even drawn.

"Yeah! You ain't shore, are you?" Rawhide sneered. "You're so goddam drunk you can't even remember how many shots you fired while you was play-actin' at being th' bold, bad gunman. I'm callin' you, Saxby, you lowdown son of a prairie rat! I'm callin' you! Lift a gun muzzle an' I'll blow th' top o' yore head off!"

A grim silence fell upon the store, a silence broken by the shuffle of feet as men pushed and shoved to get out of the line of fire.

"Make yore mind up, Saxby! You ain't got long to live anyway — now or later. Try it now — or meet me, sober,

77

at sundown. C'mon now, which'll it be?"

Silence again, a thick silence heavy with menace, until, with a sort of sob, Saxby dropped his Colts and bolted out through the back door revealed by the shifting crowd.

Rawhide hooked his thumbs in his gun belts and turned to face the thinning crowd as a gusty sigh went up.

"Me an' Saxby," he told them, "Smith he calls himself here, me an' him have a private argument. I wouldn't want any o' you jaspers hornin' in on it, an' speakin' personal I'd admire to shoot th' next funny hombre that gits to ribbin' a settler an' makin' him dance 'thout no boot-heels! Hey, Foran! C'mon in again, this here storekeeper he allows he got somethin' for you — startin' off with a new pair o' boots! Which o' you dumb clucks owns this joint?"

The crowd dispersed quickly, most of them looking reasonably foolish, and a stout man came forward.

"I'm Marsh," he announced, as if it meant something. "I own this store, an' I want to know what'n hell you think . . . "

The muzzle of one of Rawhide's Colts jarred into Marsh's belly.

"Don' think; git some boots for Foran — or maybe I'll change my mind about not shootin' you, Marsh."

"You can't do this to me! I'm a big man in this town, an' th' law . . . "

"Th' law don' allow settlers to be shot up — an' you know it. Whyn't you stop Saxby — uh, Smith? Foran, look around for a pair o' boots. Got a list you want filled? Marsh here is aimin' to have you see Mountain City recognises its mistakes an' he intends to make up for 'em!"

The storekeeper started to protest further, but Rawhide's eyes were so cold and the pressure of his gun muzzle so steady that Marsh's shoulders sagged and he turned away with the protest stillborn on his fat lips.

79

"I — I ain't got much cash, mister," Foran said uncertainly.

"Cash?" Rawhide asked. "Dinero don' buy nothin' in this store, does it, Marsh? Marsh aims to outfit you for yore journey, don' you, Marsh?"

Slowly and reluctantly Marsh nodded, hate in his eyes that were still on the Colts in Rawhide's hands. "I — I guess so," he muttered.

"Go right ahead, Foran, pick what you need, pick th' best an' pick plenty. Marsh'd be plumb disgusted if you didn't take a lot — an' git yore wimmen folks in, there'll be plenty they need." There was; Marsh got glummer and glummer as Marcia and her mother picked over his goods and added more and more to the growing pile in the middle of the floor. Mrs. Foran, a thin, complaining woman, managed to forget she was supposed to be sick for long enough to raid Marsh's shelves as thoroughly as an Apache squaw. The wagon springs creaked as Marsh's boy loaded all the goods under the tilt, and

Marsh's face was thunderous as the Forans, dazed but happy, walked out of the store with the last packages.

"I'll git even with you for this," Marsh told Rawhide, through clenched teeth.

"You're better'n even awready," Rawhide replied acidly. "You been gyppin' settlers for years, an' now one family's gotten some of its own back. Maybe you ain't been breakin' th' law, Marsh, but I got a dang good mind to snag you on a bullet all th' same. Play it a bit careful in future, feller!" He backed out of the store, round to the offside of the wagon.

"I — I don' know how to thank you, mister," Foran spluttered.

"Don't. It was a pleasure."

"That man — Saxby you called him — why did you — what did you mean when . . . ?"

"When I gave him till sundown? I jus' don' wanta kill him drunk!"

"Kill him?"

Rawhide looked up into Marcia's

eyes and saw horror in them.

"That's right, ma'am," he said quietly. "That feller done me plenty dirt — he ain't fit to live."

"That's as maybe; but who appointed you to be his executioner?"

"Why, me. I appointed myself, ma'am. There ain't no law kin take care o' what he done to me." Rawhide had to make a distinct effort to turn his eyes away from the girl's troubled ones. "Foran," he said, "this wagon o' yourn needs plenty attention. Drive on up street a few blocks. There's a saddlers an' harness-makers there."

"But I ain't got no money for no new harness an' I can't take . . . "

"I'm payin' for this," Rawhide stated.

"But why should you help us?" the girl demanded. There was pride in her voice, pride and more than a hint of anger. "We're not paupers, we can look after ourselves!"

"Lady, not out here you can't, an' not on th' Journada. Yore outfit's gotta be right for that or you jus' ain't got a dawg's chance o' gettin' through."

"But you haven't answered my question."

"Why should I help you? Guess I ain't shore myself, but I always was a sucker for things as couldn't help themselves — an' you had a tough deal in th' west. Folks are mos'ly purty nice out here — an' honest too."

"We ain't takin' no help from a man that intends to break the Lord's Commandments!" Mrs. Foran's voice was sharp and metallic.

Rawhide looked up into her hot, accusing eyes. "Ma'am," he said, "I guess we all of us have broke one o' them Commandments from time to time."

"'Thou shalt not kill', says the Good Book. Me an' mine ain't gonna be beholden to killers!"

"Mother, there ain't no call to be rude to Mister — Mister . . . "

"Storm's my name — Rawhide Storm folks mos'ly call me, an' I'm a hard man to be rude to. Pull up,

Miss, we're there!"

Stan Kayll, the saddler, was just as willing to gyp settlers as the other traders of Mountain City, but Rawhide's sharp voice and steely eyes were enough to make him change his mind about the Foran family. He routed out a set of secondhand harness in reasonable condition and at a reasonable price. After that, Rawhide made Foran drive to the wheelwright's, where Jim Webb agreed reluctantly to take the wagon in hand and have it properly redded up in a couple of days. Then Rawhide escorted the Forans to Dowd's Hotel, where, after some argument, a couple of rooms were placed at their disposal. While the women set about tidying themselves Foran took a rocker beside Rawhide on the porch.

"I can't pay for any o' this," he began diffidently.

Rawhide rolled a cigarette and touched a match to it; for all his indolent pose he was keenly alert. Saxby had been badly scared, but there was just a chance his fright might have sobered him sufficiently to enable him to use a rifle. Probably he was sleeping off his drunken state, but it could be he was waiting for an opportunity to anticipate sundown.

"Them cayuses o' yourn," Rawhide said at last. "They ain't no use."

Foran lifted his thin shoulders helplessly. "I know, but they're all I've got."

Rawhide drew smoke deep into his lungs, then let it trickle out. He wanted to help Foran, but the little man had shown courage facing Saxby and Rawhide didn't want to hurt the pride that hid behind Foran's diffidence. Foran would need all his pride and courage when he came to the Journada.

"I'm figgerin' I might git to Californy sometime," he said slowly, "an' I heard tell that mules is right scarce there."

"Reckon mules had oughta be purty cheap here!" Rawhide smoked in silence for some while, his eyes attracted by a suspicious movement of the blind still drawn across the window of the *Welcome* saloon across the street. He thought he saw an eye peering at him from round the edge of it. "Yeah," he said slowly, "guess I'll take me a look around, an' if I do pick out a team maybe you'd use 'em for me, huh?"

"Use 'em? How?"

"Use 'em to pull yore wagon across th' Journada — they're stronger than hawsses an' don' drink so much."

"I ain't never handled mules," Foran said doubtfully.

"Jarheads ain't difficult, you jus' gotta let 'em know who's boss an' keep outa th' way o' their hoofs — jarhead kicks quicker'n a rattlesnake strikes."

Foran cleared his throat. Rawhide noticed that his thin, worn hands were intertwining nervously.

"I — I'm grateful," he said, "plumb grateful, but I — we can't take no help from you. We took too much awready. I don' want you should think I'm takin' any notice o' what Ma said — I ain't!

I — I ain't — I mean — far's I'm concerned a man's gotta play things th' way he figgers best. There ain't a lot o' law out here an' — an' if I caught th' feller that stole my cash in Denver I'd shoot him. But no more help!"

"Shucks! I wouldn't be helpin' you with th' mules — you'd be helpin' me. I'd have me a stake in Californy if ever I need it, an' that's a right big thing."

"You're jus' tryin' to disguise yore help — an' you know it. Why should you help us, anyway?"

Rawhide pitched away the stub of his cigarette, then rolled and lit another. "Dunno quite," he admitted. "I been tryin' to figger it out my own self. Funny, las' six months I had plenty o' trouble an' didn't git much help. You had plenty o' trouble too; guess I kinda figured . . . Hell, I dunno." His voice trailed away and no word was spoken for some minutes until Foran said:

"Maybe I know how you feel. I — we

certainly could do with some help. I was beginnin' to think Janet had made a big mistake havin' me sell up in Ohio an' trail all th' way out west, but she's sick, an' I hoped . . . "

"Yeah, shore. C'mon, let's go see if th' livery stable's gotten any jarheads!"

Walt Andrews, the stable-keeper, had got a team of mules; he had taken them as the price of a feed bill a stalled family of immigrants hadn't been able to pay, and since none of the subsequent arrivals had had any money either and nobody in the county wanted mules he had almost begun to think he had outsmarted himself. Even so, he had an inflated idea of their worth, and Rawhide had to argue and threaten for some while before he got the six for a reasonable price.

"You're goddam lucky," he told the stable-keeper who signed the bill of sale, "you're goddam lucky to find anyone to take these jarheads offen yore han's. Yeah, make it out to David Foran — I'm buyin' for him. Here's yore three hundred bucks, an' five for their keep till Foran pulls out."

Andrews accepted the money gloomily, his manner trying to convey the impression that by making the deal he was condemning a wife and a string of children to starvation, but there was a relieved look in the back of his eyes. "Five bucks in on'y enough for a couple o' days," he grumbled. "Them jarheads eat plenty!"

"It's enough for as long as Foran wants," Rawhide replied curtly. "C'mon, Foran, time we ate!" He walked out under the livery stable arch, turned on the boardwalk to wait for Foran, and as he did so he felt a gun muzzle push into his back and heard Wiley's voice say:

"Easy, Storm! Easy. Jus' elevate yore han's!"

For one moment Rawhide stood still as a cottonwood trunk, then faced slowly round, his hand not raised but held stiffly away from his sides. A dribble of chewing tobacco trickled down from Wiley's grinning mouth.

"Up with 'em!" the marshal ordered.

"Why? What'n hell you think you're doin'?"

"Arrestin' you, Storm, that's what."

"Arrestin'? Me? What'n Tophet for?"

"Murder!" Wiley clamped his teeth on the word. "Murder, that's what."

"You crazy? I ain't murdered no one!"

"No? We figger you have. Smith got back to his cabin a while since an' found his woman dead — beat up. She was yore wife once, he says, an' we figger you done for her. You was seen to go down there this mornin'!"

Rawhide looked slowly round at the crowd which had gathered, a crowd which was clearly hostile. He looked down at the gun in Wiley's hand, Wiley's thumb on the hammer. For a fraction of time Rawhide considered going for his own guns. No, he decided, that would be suicidal. Wiley was an experienced law officer, he was sober and a practised hand with a gun.

"String him up!" a voice growled from the back of the crowd. "Lynch him!" advised a voice nearer the front. "Let's have us a necktie party!" another voice urged, and in a moment the crowd surged angrily forward, blood-eager in an instant. Wiley tried to look concerned, but didn't succeed too well.

"Get back, fellers!" he bawled. "We gotta do this 'cordin' to law an' order. Man ain't guilty till he's proved so! You comin' quiet?" he asked.

Rawhide nodded and allowed the marshal to take his guns. He saw all too well that at that moment he had no alternative. Two minutes later bolts thudded home, fastening on grilles that shut him in a cell. Wiley went back to the outer door of his office.

"C'mon you outa here, all o' you!" he ordered, and the half dozen or so eager citizens who had followed him in reluctantly departed. Wiley slammed the door behind them, bolted it, then turned back towards his prisoner.

"Run things neat in Mountain City, huh?" he queried. "You made a big mistake here, feller. You should ha' played things different. Don' pay to push fellers like Marsh around any — he don' like it."

Rawhide didn't answer. He just sat down on his plank bed and tried to think connectedly.

"Is that true about Alin?" he asked after a long silence.

"That she was beaten to death? Course it is! You should know!"

"I didn't. Saxby done it, o' course. Got back drunk an' scared — the louse — an' took it out on her."

"Your story, Storm. Your story, but you'll have a hell of a time provin' it!"

"Saxby!" Rawhide gritted his teeth. "Saxby framed me for one murder an' now he's done it again. You can't prove nothin', Wiley!"

The marshal laughed shortly and poured himself a drink from a bottle he took from his desk. "Proof? What th' hell do I want with proof?" he jeered. "Don' reckon you're gonna git no trial, do you? You made yoreself plumb unpopular in Mountain City, feller, an' we don' like jaspers goin' around sayin' we gyp folks here — it ain't good for business. Marsh an' Jim Webb an' them others, they don' like bein' made to give things away free to no broken-down settlers. Like I said, you played it all wrong!"

"So I won't git no trial, huh?"

"'Course, I shall do my duty an' stand 'em off for as long as I kin, but I can't be expected to risk my life for no prisoner — not on th' money this town pays me."

"Law officer!" Rawhide commented bitterly. "I seen better things crawlin' out from under a rotten log!"

"Ain't no use abusin' me," Wiley told him cheerfully. "You shouldn't ha' tried to buck Mountain City. It don' pay!"

5

RAWHIDE fumbled out the makings, rolled himself a cigarette, touched a match to it, swung his legs up on the bunk and lay back smoking.

"Shore am in a spot," he told himself grimly. "Maybe I have been a fool; I should ha' shot Saxby in that store. But hell! He was drunker'n Davy's sow, an' he's gotta know when he gits it, he's gotta be sober an' scared, an' suffer. Gawd! I've suffered — an' Alin, pore bitch, she must ha' suffered too. Maybe I was hard on her, but she shore done me dirt. Saxby, I'll git him somehow if it's th' las' thing I do."

He smoked on, trying to think of some way of getting out of jail; the walls of the cell were formed of thick logs roughly chinked with mud; he had a knife in his right boot, but while sharp it was thin, and even if Wiley went away — which he showed no signs of doing — Rawhide doubted whether his blade could make much impression on the seasoned pine trunks.

Noon passed and the afternoon dragged slowly on while the pile of cigarette butts rose beside the bunk. Wiley had a few drinks, ate some food brought in from the restaurant, dozed in his chair, but came awake every time Rawhide moved. The heat became oppressive, thick, heavy heat which made Wiley loosen his neckerchief and swear at the sweat which trickled down inside his shirt; he took another drink, tilting the bottle right over, and looked longingly over at the Placer.

"I could use a drink," Rawhide suggested, "an' some food. I got cash."

Wiley lurched out of his chair. "Gimme!" he said curtly. The heat and the liquor had given his face a tinge of purple, but he still had enough caution not to reach his hand in through the bars; he waited till Rawhide pushed the ten-spot through to him, when he snatched it and stumped out. He had hardly gone past the door when it opened again and Marcia Foran sidled quickly through and hurried to the cell bars.

"Did you kill that woman?" she demanded as Rawhide swung off the bunk to reach his side of the bars in one stride.

"I didn't," he said.

Her breast heaved as she drew a deep breath and some of the anxiety went out of her grey eyes.

"They — they say you did, but I . . ."

"I didn't. First I heard of it was when Wiley put th' arm on me. You gotta believe me, Marcia!"

A faint flush crept up her neck at his first use of her christian name. "I — I believe you," she told him. "But there's talk . . . Was she your wife?"

"Yeah. She ran off with Saxby; they

framed me for murder."

"They what? Your own wife? But how . . . ?"

"Saxby mus' be one smooth feller — an' clever too."

"They're saying that they'll . . . " She stopped, confused, looking away.

"They're gonna lynch me? So Wiley was kind enough to tell me. Hell of a law officer he is! I guess Marsh an' Webb an' them others are spendin' plenty on liquor now, gettin' th' boys in th' right frame o' mind."

"And if you hadn't helped us — interfered — on our behalf . . . ?"

"Shucks! Don' never worry about that, man does what he figgers is right — too bad if it turns out wrong. I should ha' guessed Wiley was on th' crook."

She fumbled at the waist of her dress. "Here," she said, "I — I brought this — it's Dad's. I dunno if it works!"

Through the bars Rawhide took an old, heavy Frontier model Colt; for a moment he gripped it, unable to say a word. "Shore swell o' you," he muttered as he pushed the weapon inside his shirt. "You're takin' an awful chance."

"I — I been watchin' th' jail for hours. I . . . "

"What'n blue blazes you doin' here?" Wiley stumbled through the door, a bottle of whisky under one arm and a food pail in one hand. "It's agin th' law to talk to prisoners. Git outa here, you — you . . . !"

"You call her one bad word an' I'll tear yore windpipe out," Rawhide snarled, and there was so much savage threat in his voice that Wiley recoiled — half drunk though he was, for he had evidently had one or two while out on his errand. However, the whisky helped him to recover his poise quickly.

"You won't be tearin' out no windpipes, Storm," he snapped back. "Likely you'll be tryin' to tear out yore own when th' rope bites."

"So you're in it too?" Marcia turned on him and fairly flung the words. "You — an officer of the law — condoning murder!"

"Lady, I dunno them big words, an' if you'll take a word of advice you'll keep yore purty trap shut! This is one tough town." He put the bottle and food on his desk, hitched up his gun belts and pushed his hat to the back of his head. "Yeah," he repeated, "purty is right. How's about a kiss, seein' you're in my office, huh?" For all his bulk he stepped quickly towards her, arms outstretched, but was met by a full arm swing with all the strength of her vigorous young body behind it, a swing which left the angry impression of her fingers on the marshal's blotched face and jarred him to his heels. Before he could recover his balance she had gone.

"Shore knocked you for a loop, fatso!" Rawhide jeered, "but it ain't nothin' to what I'll do to you if you make a pass at that gal again."

"You ain't never gonna do nothin' to nobody agin!" Wiley bawled, "an' jus' for that you don' git no food!"

"Bring it over here," Rawhide ordered sharply, "an' pronto! Or I'll shore as hell drill you!"

Wiley gaped at the Frontier Colt in Rawhide's hand. "That bitch!" he breathed. "That goddam bitch! She slipped you that gun."

"Don' never no matter where I got it — it aims to blow a hole in yore belly less'n you unlock this door. C'mon, Wiley, I ain't got for ever!"

The colour faded from the marshal's face, the pallor grotesque against the whisky blotches; for a moment it looked as though he was going to do as he was told. He reached out a hand towards the hook on which the keys hung, then he let his hand fall away from the hook.

"Hell, no!" he said, his voice far from level. "Hell, no, won't do you no good to shoot me, Storm, no dang good at all you plug me, you can't git at th' keys, an' a shot'll bring th' boys a-runnin' . . . " He went on

100

talking quickly, almost wildly, as much to convince himself as for any other reason; Rawhide cursed savagely — but under his breath. Wiley was quite right when he said that a shot would bring the boys running — Rawhide had known that well enough. Where he had been wrong had been in thinking that Wiley wouldn't have the nerve to remember that when he was looking down the muzzle of a Colt.

"Shut yore trap an' do as you're told!" Rawhide snapped. "Maybe th' boys would come fast, but it wouldn't help you with a slug through that fat belly o' yores, takes th' hell of a time to die that away an' hurts worse'n Apache torture."

"You can't scare me," Wiley blustered, not entirely convincingly, as Rawhide trained the muzzle of the Colt down to a point at the pit of Wiley's bulging stomach; as he squinted along the sights it struck him that the light had become very bad all of a sudden, the heat was more oppressive than ever, seeming to bear down upon him with an almost tangible weight. Sweat trickled down his forehead, down his neck, inside his shirt.

"I'm gonna give you five seconds, Wiley," he said, "an' then I'm gonna pull th' trigger." He gritted, "five seconds, an' then I'm gonna shoot me a crooked law officer, th' which same is somethin' I've always been honin' to do. Five seconds, an' I'll blow a hole in yore belly you could put yore head in. One — two — three . . . "

The small office became darker and darker, and as Rawhide reached 'four' and was wondering whether to carry out his threat or not, the darkness was riven by a fantastically jagged flash of lightning followed on the instant by an appalling crash of thunder. Rawhide saw Wiley dive for the door before the darkness shut down more intensely than before, darkness once again slashed by flash after flash as the storm got into its thunderous stride, rain and hail lashed down, forcing its way instantly through the badly chinked roof, and before he knew what was happening Rawhide was soaked to the skin — and the cap and ball Colt he held was useless, caps and powder both ruined by the wet.

For a moment or two he slumped back on the bunk, cursing violently as the storm raved and ranted overhead, then he pushed the useless Colt into his waistband, pulled out his knife and as a last resort attacked the weakest log he could find, with a fury he was careful to control. Almost at once he knew he had little hope of cutting a way out, for the wood was tough; it could be only a matter of minutes before Wiley was back with help; Wiley couldn't know that Rawhide's Colt was useless, but he would have no answer to a rifle pushed through the window opposite the cell. He carved and cut, afraid all the time the blade would break, one ear lifting among the thunder crashes for the sound of the door. He heard it creak before he had penetrated more than a couple of inches into the log he'd selected, and whipped round, gripping the Colt, ready to make what resistance he could — and saw Marcia Foran by the light of a lightning flash. The rain had plastered her hair to her head and soaked her thin dress which clung to her figure.

"I heard what happened," she told him. "Where's the key?" She flinched as a clap of thunder exploded, it seemed only yards overhead. Her teeth were chattering with fear, but she reached the bunch of keys indicated by Rawhide's pointing finger and managed to get back to the cell door.

"Quick! They'll soon be back!" she urged, scared that in her obvious terror she would drop them; she fumbled with the keys, her hands trembling violently. "I can't stand storms," she muttered.

Rawhide reached through the bars, took the keys, found the one he wanted and managed to twist his wrist round far enough to turn it; the click was one of the most welcome sounds he had ever heard. Outside the cell in a moment, he got an arm round the girl just in time to prevent her falling to the floor in a dead faint. Swearing again, he carried her over to Wiley's chair, pushed her head down between her knees before he grabbed his own Colts from the desk drawer where Wiley had left them.

In a moment or so Marcia showed signs of life, her eyes opened and she winced as another flash ripped the darkness, a flash which revealed Wiley and three other men at the opening door. Rawhide drew and fired into the thick planks of the closed door. "C'mon," he urged the girl, "git over under th' window, for now it's th' on'y place they can't reach."

Bullets ripped through the window, raking the place where they had stood only seconds before. Rawhide barred the door and replaced the cartridges he had used. "We gotta git outa here," he said.

Marcia managed a shaky laugh. "I

was thinkin' th' same thing," she replied. "Don' seem like I helped much."

Rawhide squeezed her hand. "If we git outa here you'll ha' saved my life, an' even if we don' — I'm plumb grateful; I shore wish you wasn't here, though."

"That ain't much of a compliment."

"Ain't no time for compliments, an' I dunno any anyway — what I mean is them buzzards'll kill you for shore if you don' git away."

"Kill me? But I thought . . . "

"Wimmen was respected out west? Yeah, shore they are, but you done poked yore nose in where it didn't fit. I'm jus' hopin' they didn't see you when they looked in. But then Wiley knows you brung me that gun. Hell an' damnation!"

In the sudden silence that followed one roll of thunder, he heard a voice outside — Marsh's voice. "I got some giant powder in my store; Stan, go an' git a couple o' sticks an' some sulphur matches — they'll do for short fuses."

Then came Wiley's voice, a bit scared. "You ain't gonna use that stuff, Marsh?"

"Why not? If he don' come out!"

A floorboard creaked under Rawhide's thigh as he moved uneasily, realising that the men outside were not aware that Marcia had come back, and as the board creaked an idea shot into his brain; he cursed because he hadn't thought of it before; he rolled over, found the end of a board with his fingers, cut out a finger-hold with his knife and prised it up; the second board was easier, and in a minute he whispered, "This way out, lady," and helped her down into the foot-high space between the floor and the earth.

"Are there any snakes under here?" she asked as he eased down beside her.

"Could be, but they're a better chance to take than that giant powder."

Rawhide felt her shivering beside him

and put an arm round her shoulders.

"I — I can't move! I hate snakes!"

"An' you're scared o' thunderstorms? Quite a gal. Yet you'll take th' risk o' fetchin' me a gun?"

"That was different."

"A dang sight more dangerous. C'mon now, follow me!" He wriggled across under the marshal's office to the back where the lightning flashes showed him an opening between the logs where a crooked timber left him just enough room to squeeze through. Rawhide helped the girl out and up to her feet in the pouring, lashing rain; for a couple of moments he held her close, trying to check her trembling, then he said, "C'mon, this ain't no place for us!"

Keeping an arm round her, he hurried away back from the marshal's office to the scrub-clad slope behind; once under cover he breathed more easily, but, realising that the girl was chilled to the bone, he hustled her on. They had to force their way through the scrub, the lightning showing the path, right up round the Maverick saloon, for he dared not risk crossing the street nearer the office with all the flashes making it as bright as day.

Eventually, after waiting immediately until after a flash, they crossed the street down which water was already flooding, opposite Dowd's Hotel, and as they did so Rawhide looked down towards the marshal's office, saw it erupt in flame and heard the roar of dynamite drowned in the crash of thunder.

"So that's th' sort o' bastards they are," he muttered. "Blow a feller to bits jus' 'cause he made 'em see what sort o' skunks they are." He helped Marcia up to the hotel porch. "Go fetch yore dad," he told her. "You gotta git outa town — pronto!"

She went inside while he crouched by the door; Dowd was far too uncertain a factor for Rawhide to chance being seen; in a few minutes Foran came sidling out followed by Mrs. Foran.

Rawhide got to his feet and put all the persuasion he could into his voice.

"Foran, you gotta git outa town!" he urged.

"B — but why? On a night like this? An' th' wagon . . . "

Rawhide fumbled some damp notes out. "Here," he said, "buy a new wagon, git yore traps shifted. You got all th' stores you want, you got harness, mules, now for Gawd's sake git outa town!"

"Storm, I don't like yore tone," Mrs. Foran interposed. "I dunno who you think you are to order my husband about that way, but I ain't takin' orders from a low-livin' man like you!"

"Lady, have sense!" Rawhide pleaded.

"Sense, is it? Sense? Seems like some'un around here oughta have some sense! You been interferin' too much with us, an' I don' like it!"

"Mother, Storm has his reasons, I — I'm shore he has."

"Yeah, probably he has, an' I don' like 'em! I seen th' way he looked at

110

Marcia. We may be poor, but we don' want no charity. We'll leave town when we think fit!"

"Leave tonight," Rawhide told her curtly, "or see yore daughter hung!"

"What you mean?" she demanded shrilly. "What you mean?"

"I mean jus' that. Marcia helped me outa jail, an' th' crooked sidewinders that run this burg know it! Now will you git?"

"Really, Mother, I — I think we oughta . . ."

"I ain't leavin' tonight — an' that's flat!"

Rawhide stepped forward and slapped her hard — once, twice. She lurched back against the door, mouth open.

"You — you hit me! Me! A sick woman!"

"Yeah, an' I'll do it again. If yore husban' had done it a few times twenty years ago maybe you wouldn't be th' dang stupid woman you are now. Go pack yore traps — an' pack 'em fast!"

"There ain't nobody ever spoke to me

like that afore. Foran, are you gonna stand by a' see yore wife insulted? An' her a sick woman too!"

"Sick woman be danged!" Rawhide cut in harshly. "Git wise to yorself, Miz Foran. You ain't sick no more'n a mountain cat, you're tough as ol' boots. I seen your sort afore, throw a wingding every time you git crossed so's your folks is too danged scared o' makin' you sick ever to do anythin' you don' want 'em to. 'T'was yore fault you ever lef' Ohio, an' for all th' good you done you could ha' stayed there, you ol' pickle-puss!"

"Why, dang you!" she burst out.

"Swearin', too," he jeered. "Have some sense, ma'am, this town is dangerous!"

"Awright," she replied shakily, "awright. I guess maybe I been selfish. I — I'm sorry, Foran, I got you inta this mess. I'll go pack our traps."

Foran's slack mouth gaped open as she went back inside the hotel.

"Wa'al," he gasped, "wa'al, tie me

an' eat me for potlikker! Gee willikens! But I'll bet she takes it out on me later."

Rawhide laughed curtly. "Jus' see she don'," he advised. "Speak to her like I done an' slap her."

Foran looked doubtful. "Easy for you, you ain't married to her. Guess you wouldnt' treat Marcia so if she was yore wife!"

"She ain't," Rawhide reminded him; but the thought rambled round in his brain and he had to force himself to concentrate. "Go git yore new wagon," he ordered, "an' fast! Storm's passin' an' it'll be light again soon."

"What are you gonna do?"

"Don' worry none about me — I got things to do, an' like I said maybe I'll see you in Californy."

"But, Storm, them mules, I dunno about mules not none at all. Could . . . "

Rawhide sighed. "Yeah, I guess so. I'll come an' help. C'mon."

The storm was passing as they went down the street, the flashes of lightning were far less frequent, the thunder-crashes less violent, but the rain still lashed down in a near solid curtain and it was still almost dark; from the stable entrance they looked down towards the marshal's office where, in spite of the rain, smoke still spiralled from the wreckage.

"They reckon they got me," Rawhide said grimly, "an' now they gone off for a drink without botherin' to find out."

Andrews was in his little cubby-hole of an office, fuddled by the best part of a bottle of whisky he'd drunk to keep out the wet.

"Whadda hell you want?" he demanded, poking his head out from under the tarpaulin which protected him from some of the water streaming through the roof.

"Them mules," Rawhide replied. "Foran's pullin' out — he reckons yore town stinks!"

Andrews bleared at him, and Rawhide could almost see the thoughts passing through his sodden brain; he had obviously been told that Rawhide had 'been taken care of' and now he planned on beating Foran out of the price of the mules.

"Them mules ain't ready to move tonight," he mumbled thickly after a long pause.

"No?" Rawhide queried roughly. "Awright, if they ain't we'll take six hawsses instead. You swore them mules was sound on'y hours gone . . . An' leave that gun alone!" A Colt seemed to leap into Rawhide's hand as he wrenched the tarpaulin away to disclose Andrews' fingers stealing towards a drawer. "C'mon, git a lantern an' make it fast!"

Grumbling under his breath, Andrews struggled uncertainly to his feet. "Lantern's outside," he said, and lurched towards the door. If he hadn't been too drunk to make the opening first time he would have done what he set out to do — get away and raise the town; as it was one shoulder struck a doorpost and put him off balance so that he nearly fell down the steps leading to the archway. Rawhide slammed his gun back in its holster, jumped for the liveryman, grabbed him just as he reached the street and choked his shout of "Hey! Wiley!" back in his throat. He then dragged him, kicking and struggling, back into the cubby-hole, held him up and exploded a right-hand punch on his jaw that slumped him on the floor like a half empty bag of meal.

"Y — you can't do that!" Foran quavered.

"I done it, ain't I? We gotta git away. C'mon!" Rawhide found the lantern, lit it and led the way to the mule stalls. With only halters he had a damnable job getting the mules out. They didn't like the wet, they didn't like the thunder, they didn't like his firm pull on their mouths, in fact they had no intention of being taken out if they could help it and showed their unwillingness in no uncertain way, their flailing hoofs completely wrecking two stalls and nearly bringing the whole roof down when they loosened an already shaky upright. Luckily the storm had circled back again and the racket they made attracted no attention. At last Rawhide got them quietened, but before he let Foran lead them out he found some rope, tied Andrews securely and dumped him behind some straw bales. As he was following the mules out a big, black horse nickered at him; he paused, rubbing his chin.

"I ain't gonna be able to fly outa here," he reminded himself. "Let's have a look at you, feller. Yeah, quite a feller, ain't you? Big quarters, shoulders, but lean hocks. You should be a flyer an' you don' seem badtempered not none. No brand either. Let's have us a look at Andrews' stock book, huh?"

The stock book disclosed that Andrews had bought the black, Dancer, for eighty dollars. Rawhide pulled out a hundred-dollar bill, pinned it to the book and scrawled a short note. "Bastard'll say I stole him," he muttered, "but I can't help that. Hawss stealin' don' stack up to murder, anyway!" He rummaged out a couple of blankets and a centre fire hull, saddled up Dancer and led him out after Foran. The big black followed docilely enough although he skittered a bit as the rain lashed down on him.

"Easy, feller!" Rawhide told him. "You're my hawss now an' you gotta do things th' way I want." His voice quietened the scared horse and they soon overtook Foran, who was having some trouble with the mules.

"Lam into 'em!" Rawhide advised. "Soon's they plumb convinced you're th' boss they'll do as you say!"

Foran lammed into the jarheads as hard as he could, and even managed a mild oath or two which carried them on as far as the wheelwright's yard where Jim Webb sat under a lean-to chewing tobacco and staring gloomily at the Foran wagon. He turned his quid and spat raggedly through his drooping moustache when he saw Foran.

"It ain't ready yet," he grumbled. "It ain't ready, an' what's more I ain't even touched it."

Rawhide ignored him, let Dancer stand with the reins over his head and began poking about in the wagon sheds; in the far back corner he found a Conestoga that was apparently in poor shape but which he believed was fundamentally sound.

"Wanna sell this, Webb?" he bawled.

"That ain't for sale," Webb yelled back, after another sprayed discharge of tobacco juice.

"Who's is it?"

"Belongs to Marsh."

"Fair enough. C'mon, Foran, gimme a hand gettin' it out!"

As they started clearing away some of the rubbish that blocked in the Conestoga, Webb came running out.

"Hey! That's Marsh's wagon," he warned. "You leave it alone!"

Rawhide turned on him. "Go jump in th' lake," he said. "G'wan, beat it!"

For answer, Webb dragged at his Colt, but before he could get it out Rawhide hit him a pile-driver right to the chin that sent him staggering back trying to catch up with his balance; he fetched up against a post, came back hard, swearing a blue streak, only to be met with a left to the stomach and a haymaker to the ear that folded him into the deep mud.

"I'll tie him up," Rawhide said, blowing on his bruised knuckles, "while you go an' fetch th' harness. Pronto now, it's gettin' lighter!"

As Foran hurried off, Rawhide cleared the rest of the rubbish and set about shifting the Conestoga; it was a heavy one and the wheels had sunk deep in the earth, but he managed it in the end and at last succeeded in moving it over to Foran's old wagon. He had transferred nearly all Foran's gear when they came back — all three of them carrying the traps they'd taken to Dowd's Hotel.

"Didn't see no point in goin' back

for 'em," Foran explained, "an' we snuck out th' back way too — Dowd don't know we've left."

"Swell," Rawhide told him, looking at Marcia. "Gimme a hand here an' I reckon you should be away in a couple o' minutes."

"You comin' too, Storm?" Marcia asked, putting a hand to his arm.

"Maybe," he replied, squeezing her hand, "but not jus' yet anyway. I got things to do here."

6

RAWHIDE stood at the entrance of the wagon yard and watched the Foran family drive away down street through the thinning rain, the mules' hoofs splashing in the foot-deep torrent flowing in the trough the street had become, the wagon lurching as its broad-tyred wheels hit the ruts; for a moment or so he was full of a sense of relief that he had got them safely away from a town that had become dangerous for them. The sense of relief passed quickly and he found himself almost regretting their departure, found he wanted to see them again — or at least he wanted to see Marcia again.

"Don' be a danged idjet," he advised himself. "Wimmen ain't brung you nothin' but grief — so leave 'em be; jus' snap out of it, feller, an' git after Saxby!"

The rain was easing off fast, the clouds were passing over and a watery, sinking sun sent pale shafts of light down the dripping street. Rawhide squinted up at the sky. "Hour to sundown," he muttered. My bet is Saxby'll try to gulch me — if he's sobered up. But, hell, he'll figger I'm dead! I'll have to figger a way out that'll plumb surprise him!" He pulled his hat low over his forehead, swung into Dancer's saddle and sent the big horse splashing down the street; people were beginning to emerge from the houses and stores, but they were more interested in talking about the storm and the damage it had done than pay any attention to the single horseman; hardly anyone looked round and certainly no one saw Rawhide swing out of the saddle and tie the horse in a patch of scrub just beyond the last house in town — the 'Smiths' cabin.

Rawhide eased up on the cabin carefully, keeping it between him and the next buildings. The door hung open and the wind and rain had beaten into the squalid, single room on which it gave; Rawhide set his teeth and went in quickly, his hand on a gun; sighing gustily with relief when he found that the cabin was empty. He had expected that Alin's body would be there — but it wasn't. Evidently someone had already arranged for it to be taken away. He stood in the centre of the poorly furnished place, his eyes bleak as he took in the evidence of the straits to which Saxby's drunken improvidence had reduced the couple. A rumple of dirty, blood-stained bedclothes showed where Alin had died, the bed still showed the impress of her body while the sagging apology for a wardrobe still showed her remaining stock of clothes. Rawhide recognised all of them; it appeared Saxby hadn't bought her any since the Hawksbee days, and the muscles of Rawhide's jaw tightened at the thought.

"Poor bitch," he muttered. "Maybe

it was my fault — or some of it."
And then he remembered Denton, the
recollection driving compassion out of
his heart. There still remained the
problem of finding Saxby. As he moved
slowly out of the dismal cabin into
the bright evening sunlight, Rawhide
dragged his hat lower over his eyes and
pulled his scarf up over his chin. Heat
had returned to the town and steam
rose from the street and from the roofs,
the few horses which had been tied to
hitch rails shook their soaked coats and
stamped in the mud.

Rawhide found himself a shadowed
corner and tucked himself into an angle
between the Snake Bite and Ed Merry's
gunsmith shop, then settled down to
wait. He didn't wait long before he
saw Wiley emerge from the Placer
and steer an uncertain course across
street to Marsh's store; the law officer
walked with grave dignity but poor
direction, lifting his feet very high
as if stepping over foot-high wires.
In front of Marsh's store he pushed

his hat to the back of his head, hit his forehead, then, after swaying uncertainly on his feet for a moment or so, he trained himself round and aimed himself at Dowd's Hotel. Dowd was half-heartedly sweeping water out on to his porch, the roof having given way somewhere. Rawhide saw Wiley lurch up to the hotel-keeper and talk with him for a few minutes, then he swung round again and headed back towards the store, walking with even more elaborate care than before, an expression of drunken disbelief on his face.

Rawhide took a chance, crossed the street a few yards behind Wiley and leant by the door after the law officer had gone inside the store.

"They done went," he heard the marshal tell Marsh.

"Done went? Who?"

"Them Forans!"

"Nuts! How could they?"

"Dowd says they have. Roof leaked in th' room he gave 'em, an' water poured through. He went up to see what they was doin' an' they wasn't."

"Wasn't what?"

"Wasn't doin' nothin'. Tol' you, did'n I? How'n Tophet could they be doin' somethin' when they don' went? Say, Marsh, I need a drink!"

"You had too much awready. C'mon in th' back room, this needs to be studied over. Here, hold up!" A pile of buckets went over with Wiley, and an infernal clatter.

"Them dang buckets," denounced the marshal from the floor, "they jus' 'liberately moved over an' tripped me up. Whaffor you got performin' buckets, Marsh?"

"I ain't! Git up, you drunken slob!"

There was a further clattering of buckets and Rawhide used the diversion to ease into the store and conceal himself behind a stack of bolts of gingham.

"Shore is funny way things trip me up," Wiley grumbled as he kicked the last bucket clear.

"Shut yore yap! Webb's here." Rawhide saw Marsh go into the back room, followed by Wiley, who slammed the door so hard it bounced back from the jamb and came to rest a couple of inches open so that he heard quite clearly Webb saying:

"Dang fine law officer you are! Drunk as Danny's sow again!"

"I kin do my job drunk or sober," Wiley averred. "Whersh th' bo'le, Marsh?"

"Here, help yoreself! Sooner you pass right out, the better we'll git on."

"I resent tha'. I ain't in th' habit o' passin' out an' I . . . "

"Aargh, shut up!" Webb snapped. "What's this about th' Forans pullin' out?"

"Wiley says they've gone — an' they've took near four hundred bucks worth o' my stock with 'em! I don' like it, Webb; they didn't 'pear to me to be th' sort o' people would pull out in that storm, more likely to put their heads under th' bedclothes."

"Shore like to have gotten my head under th' bedclothes with th' daughter," Wiley said thickly.

"Thought I tol' you to shut up!" Webb snarled at him. "You dang, stupid idjet! Don' you see what this means?"

"Means? Why, 'course I do! Them Forans didn't like yore smell, Webb — so they pulled their freight!"

"My freight," Marsh reminded him bitterly.

"An' in yore wagon," Rawhide muttered to himself, from the point behind the door to which he had moved.

"What Webb means," Marsh went on, "is that Storm musta got 'em outa town."

"Storm? He's dead! Blown plumb to smithereens!"

"Ah! Is he?"

"Whaddya mean? 'Course he's dead! Danged office o' mine was wrecked, wasn't it?"

"We didn't find no body."

"Didn't look hard, did we? With all that rain — an' like I said ther'd on'y be bits!"

"Go an' have a look now!" Marsh ordered.

"Go look yore ownself! Storm's cashed in his chips — an' goo' riddance too! We oughta be able to git th' money for his lan' outa Smith now."

"Gawd, how dumb kin you git? Smith on'y got that dinero from his woman, an' now she's dead . . ."

"Maybe," Webb cut in swiftly, "but ain't nobody outa this town knows it, huh? That Hawksbee place is a good way off, an' that Eastern jasper ain't gonna look too close at no signature on a bill o' sale."

"Maybe you got somethin' there," Marsh replied. "Where at is this Smith feller? Saxby, Storm called him."

"Gettin' stewed in th' Placer. What for we want him?"

"Yeah, shore. Ain't no reason to

cut him in on this. We'll git it direct 'stead o' takin' it offen him at poker later. Yeah, shore that ranch o' Storm's oughta be worth plenty!"

Rawhide kicked the door full open and lounged into the room.

"It was, you buzzards," he said quietly, "but I awready sold it!"

For an instant there was silence, then — "Hey! You're dead!" Wiley gulped. His unsteady words broke the spell; Marsh, who had been sitting with his back to the door, dived sideways out of his chair as Webb's right hand streaked for a shoulder-holster and Wiley fumbled for the Colt on his hip. Rawhide's hands dropped to his Colts with the speed of a swooping hawk, the guns came swiftly up to the level in smooth, unerring arcs, belched flame and smoke, their explosions thunderous in the small room. Hit dead centre, Webb was jerked over backwards in his chair by the impact of the bullet that killed him. Wiley, his right shoulder shattered, tried to regain his balance, tried and tried in vain, then slid sideways to the floor as consciousness left him. Colts smoking in one hand, Rawhide told Marsh who, squirming round trying to reach the gun Wiley had dropped.

"I wouldn't, feller," Rawhide advised quietly. Marsh turned his ashen face upwards, his mouth working as if he was trying to prevent himself from being sick.

"Git up!" Rawhide ordered. He had to yank the store-keeper to his feet, for all Marsh's bluster and brag had been jerked out of him by the two shots. "Set down there, if you can't stand," Rawhide went on, and shoved him into a chair as feet pounded into the store and a voice demanded:

"You got trouble, Marsh?"

Rawhide kicked shut the door of the inner room.

"Speak up, Marsh, an' tell him Wiley was fiddlin' with a gun — he was drunk!"

Marsh gulped, his lips moving

soundlessly until a menacing lift of a Colt muzzle helped him to find his voice.

"It's awright, Zach," he said.

"Louder!" Rawhide urged.

"It's awright, Zach!" Marsh croaked. "Wiley's drunk; got to foolin' with his gun; no trouble."

"Aw. Sorry, Marsh," said the voice, and the feet tramped away.

"Wouldn't ha' worried me shootin' you, Marsh," Rawhide told him, "but I wouldn't ha' wanted to shoot Zach as well, this is none o' his put in."

Marsh licked his lips, his hands slack beside him as he sat slackly in his chair.

"You — you ain't gonna shoot me?"

"Don' see why not; you ain't no better than them other buzzards 'cept you don' pack a gun an' you didn't pull one. Crooked law officers are lower'n a snake's belly."

Marsh pulled himself up a bit. "You come here lookin' for Saxby?"

"Ain't news, is it?"

"'Naw, but I kin help you git him easy. He's in th' Placer, an' if you use th' door I'll tell you about you'll come in behind where he stands. I knew some'un was lookin' for him 'cause he always sits an' stands where he kin see th' door, an' he's always practising' pullin' his guns . . . " The gabbling voice died away as Marsh saw the contempt in Rawhide's eyes.

"You," Rawhide told him, "are jus' about th' meanest horswogglin' toad I ever did meet in all my borned days. Why, you ain't even fit to have lice!" He shoved his guns back in their holsters and, the moment he no longer had to stare into their menacing muzzles, Marsh recovered some of his nerve.

"I almost stood about enough from you, Storm," he retorted. "I awready stood more from you than I ever stood afore from anyone. Now git outa my store 'fore I throw you out!"

Rawhide chuckled. "Lookit who's talkin'," he said. "For a feller that had th' shakes a moment ago you shore perk up prompt. I'm through with you, Marsh, an' I'm leavin' — but not afore I've made good an' shore you don' bother me none again. You got a cellar?"

"Shore I gotta cellar. But what . . . "

"Show me it. I'm leavin' you there, Marsh. I don' trust you no further than I could push back a Mogul!"

"Lock me up? In my own cellar! Hell, no!" Marsh's attack was so sudden. He bounced up from his chair so quickly that Rawhide was taken by surprise and collected a swing to his chin that rattled his teeth and fogged his brain for a moment, a moment in which Marsh drove home a vicious left to Rawhide's stomach. Rawhide shook his head to clear it, then backed away from the flurry of punches the store-keeper flung at him, blocking most and riding others until Marsh left himself wide open to a wicked right that landed behind his left ear and toppled him to the floor.

"Dang fool!" Rawhide muttered,

rubbing his bruised belly. "He shore had a dig for a fat man, an' I dunno where his cellar is." However, he compromised by tying Marsh up with his own and Webb's belts, gagging him with his suspenders. He locked the door on the way out, throwing the key away in the deep mud of the dark street as he crossed it towards the Placer. Outside the saloon he hesitated, came to a stop, strangely uneasy now that the long trail of Saxby seemed to be at an end. It seemed totally inadequate that all he had left to do was to walk into the Placer, call Saxby down, beat him to a draw and blow a hole through him. Rawhide didn't hate the fellow any longer, or any more than he hated the flies that buzzed over meat and polluted it. They had to be killed just as Saxby had to be killed. They weren't fit to live — nor was he.

Rawhide shrugged slightly, checked his guns, replacing the cartridges he burnt in Marsh's store, then he settled his holsters and, with his heart beating a little faster than usual, shouldered through the swing doors into the Placer. The saloon was no more full than it had been before. In fact it looked almost as though the same poker game was going on — the rest was different. Sid, the barman, stopped as if frozen in the process of polishing a glass, which dropped from his fingers and smashed on the walnut counter. Saxby, sitting on a bar stool away off to one side, turned sharply at the noise, sudden pallor spreading over his face as Rawhide swung round towards him, his hands crooked over his gun butts.

"Saxby," he said, in a voice that cut like a knife, "Saxby, I'm callin' you for a low-down coyote, a wife stealin' bastard an' a murderin' skunk! Go for yore gun, buzzard meat!"

Saxby held his hands stiffly out, eased off his stool to stand half crouched.

"He's yaller," Rawhide told himself. "He's makin' a play o' bein' a gunman — but he's yaller clear through. He ain't hardly worth a cartridge."

In the tense silence of the room it was possible to hear a card drop. Saxby's breath came gustily. He was drunk again, but not as drunk as he had been the previous evening. There was a terror of death in his eyes, his hands trembled and a tic beat under his left eye.

"C'mon, Saxby," Rawhide called. "You're brave enough killin' wimmen — drag yore iron!"

There was still no move from Saxby. He seemed incapable of doing anything but gulp for breath. Rawhide moved forward, lips twisting in a sneer.

"Hell of a feller, ain't you? Figger you can't beat me to th' draw, huh? Don' fancy knowin' you been beat! C'mon, at least try an' die like a man 'stead o' th' coyote you been all yore life!"

Rawhide started to move forward again, but one foot caught in a loose board which threw him, for a moment, off balance, and in that moment Saxby moved. His hand fell like a thrown stone, his gun coming out and up before Rawhide's guns cleared leather. Realising he was being beaten to the draw, Rawhide gave up his effort to regain his balance, let his legs go limp and rolled over as Saxby's gun roared. As he fell to his right he got his left-hand gun up in time for a snap shot which blew Saxby's Colt out of his hand. Rawhide completed his roll and came smoothly up to his feet before Saxby could grab his fallen weapon.

"Hold it!" Rawhide ordered. "Shootin's too good for you!" He stepped forward, kicked Saxby's gun away and holstered his own. "I'm gonna kill you, Saxby," he said quietly. "Kill you th' hard way, with my bare hands. You're gonna suffer for all th' beatin's you got me in jail."

Slowly, never taking his eyes off the big man, Rawhide unbuckled his gun belts and handed them over the bar. "They better be waitin' for me, Sid," he stated, "'cause if they ain't I'll take you apart when I'm done with this sidewinder."

Saxby had straightened up. There was a gleam of hope in his eyes and a touch of malicious triumph Rawhide didn't miss as he moved slowly forward.

"C'mon, fight, dang you!" he gritted.

Saxby's wide mouth opened in a derisive smile. "You pore sap!" he said. "You figger I on'y carry one gun?" If he hadn't stopped to jeer Saxby could have got his underarm gun out in plenty of time, but his words gave Rawhide just sufficient warning to enable him to hurl himself at Saxby as the latter's hand streaked for his shoulder-holster.

The gun was already out when Rawhide gripped his wrist. Another splinter of a second and Saxby would have gotten it lined up. As soon as his hand closed on Saxby's wrist Rawhide knew he would require every ounce of strength. Saxby's power surprised him, for his first effort to free his wrist nearly flung Rawhide clear. Rawhide had grabbed his opponent's wrist with his left hand, which didn't give him much leverage, but he didn't dare shift hands. He smashed his right again and again into Saxby's face, feeling savage exultation as bone and flesh crunched under his knuckles. He heard Saxby grunt with pain as he landed a punch on Rawhide's head, who realised that Saxby's right hand couldn't do much damage; having had a gun blown out of it wouldn't have improved it as a weapon, and from that moment on Rawhide knew he was going to win.

Entirely disregarding Saxby's blows, he smashed away alternately at Saxby's face and his belly, which he guessed wouldn't be in good shape to stand much punishment after the amount of whisky that had been poured into it. Saxby didn't like it. He kept his right hand working, but each blow he struck hurt him much more than it hurt Rawhide and the knowledge that he was weakening showed in what little of his eyes were still visible. Rawhide managed to work his left hand out from Saxby's wrist until he had a grip on the Colt. Gradually he gained leverage on it until, with an all-out effort, he wrenched it out of Saxby's fingers and flung it away before using both hands in vicious chopping blows that sent Saxby lurching back to the bar where he brought up with a bang. All resistance had gone out of him and he'd become no more than a chopping block for Rawhide's savage blows.

A red mist clouded Rawhide's sight; he didn't clearly see the barman push a full whisky bottle into the hand that Saxby flung on the counter. He hardly saw the bottle swing towards his head, didn't see it in time before it crashed against his skull. The blow sent him sideways, sick and dizzy, more than halfway to unconsciousness. The next blow, which smashed the bottle, knocked him to the floor. Seconds passed before his brain cleared sufficiently for him to get to his knees, shaking his head in an effort to disperse the cotton-wool fog which clogged his thoughts.

As he staggered to his feet and gripped the bar to steady himself he was dimly aware that the swing doors clashed, and it was some seconds later before he realised that Saxby had gone, that the fading pound of hoofs outside meant that he was little nearer paying his debt than he had been before he reached Mountain City. With that bitter realisation his brain cleared. He bent down, disregarding the pain that shot through his head and the blood that trickled down his neck as he picked up Saxby's short Colt and held it loosely in his hand as he said to Sid, "You give him that bottle?"

Sid backed away. "It was right by his hand."

"That's yore story, feller. Any reason why I shouldn't shoot you?"

Sid dredged up an apology for a smile. "Agin th' law," he mumbled.

"So's buttin' in on another man's

fight. Gimme my guns!"

In the silence that could be felt, Sid handed over the weapons. Rawhide buckled them on and walked out of the Placer without a backward glance, then made for the place he had left his horse.

Fifty yards or so down street he tripped over something and fell sprawling in the mud.

"Yeah," said a voice, "that makes it jus' plumb unanimous. Some jasper steals m' bronc, upends me in the mud, an' then jus' as I make up me mind to git up you come along an' tramp me back inta it again!"

Rawhide got back on his feet. "Sorry, feller," he said as he helped the aggrieved puncher to his feet. "This jasper — he come outa th' Placer?"

"Shore did, an' like he was shot from a gun. Y'see, I was jus' talkin' to my bit o' crowbait, tellin' him what I thought o' him, an' this jasper . . ."

"Yeah, shore," Rawhide interrupted the spate. "Which way did he go?"

"Why, I'm tellin' you, ain't I? He went down street — th' which same proves he's crazy — once for stealin' my hawss which ain't worth a light, bein' spavined, knock-kneed and broken-winded, an' second for headin' that way which there's on'y th' Journada at th' bottom o' th' hill."

"Thanks, feller," Rawhide said. "Here, buy yoreself a new hawss!" He folded a couple of ten-dollar notes into the puncher's top pocket and hurried off down street, eager to get Dancer and send him rocketing after Saxby on his broken-winded nag. But when he reached the patch of scrub where he had left the black horse tied he found only a knife-slashed halter and a buckskin pony standing with splayed legs and drooping head, still wheezing as a result of its quarter-mile run from the Placer.

Rawhide opened his mouth to swear then shut it with a snap. The position was far beyond even the most violent language at his command. He felt the

145

buckskin over, wincing as his probing fingers found evidence of all the faults its owner had mentioned, then he heaved himself into the saddle as carefully as possible, half fearful that the animal would fall over under his weight.

"C'mon, li'l pony," he urged gently. "We got a long way to go." The buckskin managed a fairly fast walk, but that, Rawhide soon found, was his limit. Faster he would not go — could not. Rawhide tried to prevent himself thinking of Saxby swinging forward on Dancer's long, smooth strides, making a yard for every foot the buckskin covered and laughing his head off at the march he had stolen on the man who had sworn to kill him. Rawhide set his teeth and rode on grimly, easing the buckskin as much as he could.

7

IN the days before the silver strikes played out, Bristowe had been quite a place. Being located miles out in the desert, miles from the remotest semblance of any law, there had been no brake on the town's wildness. Robbery had been an everyday occurrence, murder almost as commonplace, and it was a rare event for the maker of a strike to leave town with either cash or skin intact. Since those great days not only had the silver lodes been almost exhausted but the water supply, always uncertain, had also become steadily worse. Gradually Bristowe had sunk to being a ghost town. First the successful gamblers and swindlers had pulled out, followed by those saloon and storekeepers who had been lucky enough to unload their property on newer mugs. The prospectors had trickled away in search of new strikes until at last there were left in Bristowe only those few who had neither the money nor the energy necessary to enable them to leave, or the rather larger number who knew that sheriffs and marshals would welcome their return to civilisation. Mean, dirty, and poverty-stricken, Bristowe maintained some sort of existence which was in itself a mild triumph of the human will to survive.

Sam, who kept the only saloon in operation — no one in Bristowe had even heard his other name — Sam was no early riser, for he consumed a considerable quantity of the mescal he both manufactured and sold. "Never sell it less'n it's seven hours old, nor drink it neither," he used to say. That morning it was some hours after dawn before he dragged himself up from his apology for a bed, soused his aching head in a bucket set ready for that purpose and, after drinking the half tumbler of mescal without which he was incapable of starting the day, he lurched into the squalid filth of the saloon, his feet scuffing dust and cigarette butts as he made his unsteady way to the door through which he had thrown the last of his customers only an hour or so before dawn.

He fumbled with the fastenings, dimly pleased to note that he hadn't been too drunk to bar the door, and tottered out to drop into his ruinous rocker on the porch boards which creaked dismally under his weight. The sun heat struck down with venomous force, but Sam was so pickled in mescal he shivered even at that temperature. Suppressing his trembling, he looked idly away along the trail that, after crossing ten miles of sun-scorched sand, wound upwards to Mountain City. He looked, not because he expected to see anything, but because it was one of the things he did every morning. He blinked, looked again, then covered his eyes with his hands, peeking out through his fingers at what he saw.

Unwilling to believe it, half afraid he had at last reached the stage of actual madness to which mescal inevitably leads, he saw, coming infinitely slowly towards him, a broken-down wreck of a buckskin horse, each step an obvious effort against weariness. The buckskin had no rider, but beside it, almost encouraging it along, was a tall, lean man who also appeared to be in the last stages of exhaustion. Sam watched the pair intently. For one thing, they were the only moving objects visible in Bristowe; for another, nothing so unusual had happened in months. Slowly, painfully slowly, man and horse came towards the saloon, and as they came nearer Sam saw that the man's lips were cracked with thirst.

"Tenderfoot," he opined. "Dang fool got hisself lost on a broken-down hoss." But then he remembered that men once lost in the desert don't ever find their way out, and he noticed the wide shoulders, the hard eyes under the

150

low-pulled hat brim, the two low-slung Colts in their tied-down holsters and reversed his opinion. "Gunhawk," he told himself. "On th' run, had to leave Mountain City on th' jump — 'thout no canteen; mus' be broke if that's all th' hawss he's got!"

Man and horse at last reached the saloon. "Easy, feller," the man croaked, then his eyes turned to Sam. "Says saloon on that there notice," he said. "It mean what it says?"

Sam blinked. He didn't like the look in those eyes any more than he liked the cold, expressionless voice. This man might be in a bad way, but he was still dangerous.

"Why, shore it's a saloon," Sam replied.

"Whisky for me — water for my hawss. Pronto!"

"Ain't got no whisky, mescal is all, an' we don' serve hawsses!"

As soon as Sam had made his crack he knew he'd also made a mistake. The cold eyes became positively icy and a gun jumped into Rawhide's left hand as he said, "Save th' funnies, feller, an' fetch water!"

Sam slowly hauled himself to his feet.

"Scarce around here," he said.

"Get it!" was the implacable reply, and as Sam shambled inside he heard Rawhide say, "You'll git yore drink, ol' feller. You shore have earned it!"

Sam returned carrying a bucket of water that had served him for a number of mornings — and looked like it. However, the old buckskin didn't care. He drank as if he'd never had a drink before. Rawhide watched him, aware that Sam eyed him doubtfully meanwhile. When the water had gone Rawhide said, "Got any oats?"

Sam smiled unpleasantly, "Ain't been no oats in Bristowe for months. Ain't nobody got no dinero to buy none, an' anyway, that crowbait don't rate no oats. Ouch!" Sam found himself on his back, a rapidly swelling lump on his jaw showing how he came there.

He looked up into Rawhide's impassive face and wished once again he hadn't let his tongue say words his brain could have told him were dangerous.

"My hawss may be crowbait, but he's still got pluck, which you ain't, you lousy son of a seasick ape! You got any hay?"

Sam slowly sat up. "Out back," he mumbled. "Barn's there — may be some hay."

Rawhide nodded, left him sitting and walked the crowbait round to the barn where he found some hay that was reasonably sweet. Then, and only then, did he realise just how near collapse he was. Strangely enough, his determination not to let the buckskin die on his hands had probably been a large factor in helping him across the miles of killing desert to Bristowe. He had eaten nothing for over twenty-four hours and it seemed almost as long since he'd had a drink. He had also had a mansized fight and the fierce sun hadn't improved the feel of his bruises.

As he walked back round to the front of the saloon he felt curiously detached from reality — as if everything was happening to somebody else while he stood aside and watched. In the sleazy bar-room Sam was helping himself to recovery by means of another half glass of mescal, at which Rawhide looked with distaste.

"That right you ain't got no whisky?" he asked.

Sam half stifled a hiccough. "Sartainly we ain't got no whisky — for th' same reason we ain't got no oats. This is a ghost town, feller, not many folks an' dang little cash."

"Gimme a shot o' that rot-gut, then — an' some water!"

Rawhide took the water first. It was brackish stuff with a strong tang of alkali, but it tasted wonderful — far better than the throat-burning mescal he slung down after it. At least the alcohol cleared his head.

"Feller git here recent?" he asked, "ridin' a big, black hawss?"

"How recent?"

"Be long about midnight, maybe an hour later."

"Big feller?"

"Yeah. You seen him?"

"No, I ain't. Ain't nobody comes to Bristowe now."

"I came, didn't I?"

"Yeah, but that's different. You'd never ha' made Coyote Springs on that bronc you wasn't ridin'."

"Coyote Springs? Where's that?"

Sam looked at him curiously. "'Bout ten miles north o' here," he said. "First water on th' direct trail from Mountain City to Marl Springs. If th' feller you want had him a good hawss an' was headin' west, he'd likely go there."

"He had a good bronc — he had mine," Rawhide admitted bitterly. "Where at kin I git some food an' some sleep?"

"You got money?"

"Enough to pay for what I want."

"Corn pone an' bacon is all. We have to grow what we eat here an' we ain't got near enough water."

Rawhide took another slug of mescal to help him fight off the fog of tiredness which was submerging his brain. He ate the unappetising food Sam produced for him even though he was almost too tired to eat, then he stretched out on Sam's bed, too weary to bother about the dirt, too weary to heed the speculative look Sam directed at the pocket from which he had taken his diminished roll to pay for what he'd had.

Weary or not, trained instinct woke him some hours later when his sleeping ears picked up a sound that should not have been — the stealthy scuff of a worn shoe on dirty boards. If Sam had had any sense he would just have walked up to Rawhide as if he was going about his usual business. As it was, his careful approach woke Rawhide, and when Sam's questing hand reached for Rawhide's pants pocket it was gripped in a grip of iron, while Rawhide's other hand pushed a gun into Sam's belly.

"Like that, huh?" Rawhide grunted, then he sat up and sent Sam's flaccid body sprawling into a far corner of the room. "Git out!" Rawhide snapped, "an' stay out till I want you. Find me a feller that knows th' Journada, an' a hawss or mule to carry me. Git!"

Rid of his unwholesome landlord, Rawhide wedged a chair against the keyless door, lashed the window shut with a bit of rope and settled down to sleep again in the oven those closures had made of the room. He was still terribly tired, but for some reason or other he couldn't get back to sleep after the interruption. All the events of the last days kept passing and repassing through his brain, but the image which made the most frequent appearance was the pale oval of Marcia Foran's face as she had looked back at him from the Conestoga as it went lurching away through the slashing rain, down street towards the Journada.

A slight creak from the rickety chair he had used to wedge the door drove all such thoughts from his brain, and he was instantly keenly alert, eased himself off the bed, crossed silently to the door which, he remembered, opened into the bar-room. He pressed his ear to the door in time to hear Sam say, "He's wedged it, Lew."

Then came another voice and a rasping drawl said, "Don' never no matter, Sam, he's gotta come out sometime. Why'd he wedge th' door? S'pose he caught you tryin' to frisk him, huh?"

"Never did," Sam countered indignantly. "Cal, you git over there with yore Hawkins an' git him if Lew misses with his scattergun!"

Rawhide pursed his lips in a soundless whistle. Evidently Sam had called in some help, having failed to lift Rawhide's roll by himself. He moved back from the door, stretched to ease his cramped muscles, drew both guns and made sure they were ready for use, then unlashed his window fastenings and climbed quietly out into the yard.

He walked silently round to the front and saw, to his astonishment, that there was a horse tied to the hitch rail, not a particularly good horse but one infinitely better than the one he had left in the stable. He settled his gun belts and eased up on to the porch to lean against one door-post. For some moments the three in the bar room didn't see him. Sam leant on the bar, a glass of mescal in one hand and an ancient Remington revolver close to his other. Cal was back in a corner to Rawhide's left, his Hawkins rifle across a table, while Lew's scattergun rested on his knees.

"Howdy, gents," Rawhide said softly, and pulled his guns, the bar-room resounding with their blast as he pulled the triggers. Four shots were enough. The rifle went spinning to the floor, Sam's Remington jumped aside and smashed Sam's glass, while the scattergun — hit on the breach — broke clean in two.

"Waitin' for anyone, gents?" Rawhide

queried gently, his guns already holstered.

Sam, well upholstered with mescal, was the first to recover from his shock. He fingered his Remington with an unsteady hand, but made no move to pick it up.

"What's th' idea?" he tried to bluster. "Cain't three frien's have a drink' thout you turnin' loose?"

"Waitin' to cut loose on me?" Rawhide snapped back. "Buzzards! Which one o' you owns th' hawss outside?"

"Me," Lew growled, "but I ain't sellin'."

"Take it in greenbacks or lead," Rawhide told him, one hand suggestively near a Colt butt.

Lew swallowed hard. "Eighty bucks," he muttered.

"Eighty? Nuts!" Rawhide told him. "Forty's nearer, forty an' th' crowbait I left out back."

"That 'un ain't even worth feedin'," Lew grumbled. "I'll take fifty."

"Awright. An' gimme a bill o' sale."

Lew sneered. "Cain't write," he said.

Rawhide shrugged. "Awright," and peeled fifty off his sadly diminished roll, which was nevertheless big enough to attract the avid gaze of three pairs of disappointed eyes.

"I'm leavin' now," Rawhide told them, "an' so's none o' you jaspers git ideas — I'll be takin' this!" He crossed the saloon swiftly and picked up Cal's Hawkins, which appeared to be undamaged. Sam's Remington he likewise scooped up and threw out through the door into the deep dust outside. Sam wouldn't be able to get the gun serviceable until Rawhide was long out of range.

Rawhide left Bristowe behind him with few regrets and some relief that he was able to ride away at all. Many lone travellers had been known to vanish without trace in the near-ghost towns which dotted the west, and he had at least managed to get a better mount out of the deal. The horse was a hammer-headed, flea-bitten grey which, although it wasn't young, had still strength and endurance far beyond that of the abandoned crowbait. Rawhide felt bad about leaving the old horse to Lew's care, but there wasn't anything else he could do about it — other than shoot the animal.

8

THE trail to Coyote Springs was a trail only in name, for the way lay across the same sort of deep, loose sand Rawhide had plodded across on his way to Bristowe. The grey horse didn't like it any more than Rawhide did, and made heavy going. Rawhide slumped in the saddle, dust caking the sweat on his face and hands, dust carried down inside his shirt and levis by the trickles of sweat brought out by the fierce sun. The heat was terrific, near overpowering, and Rawhide tried to close his mind, to force it to disregard bodily discomfort, to concentrate only on the delicious prospect conjured up by the words Coyote Springs.

The sun was setting before he reached what he could only conclude were the Springs. It was, if anything, hotter than it had been at noon, for the setting sun still had force and the sand was giving up the heat it had absorbed during the day in stifling waves. A few disspirited clumps of mesquite, some poor gramma grass, some stunted greasewood and a muddy pool — that was Coyote Springs. Beside the unattractive spring there burnt a small camp fire over which hung a battered coffee pot. A frying pan with some bacon lay off to one side near a couple of pack saddles and a riding saddle. Abruptly aware that Saxby could well be looking at him over the sights of a rifle, Rawhide cursed the weariness and heat exhaustion that had allowed him to ride up so carelessly. He looked keenly round, but could see no signs of the man to whom the outfit belonged. He dismounted and let his horse drink some of the muddy water, pulling it back when he thought it had had enough. Then he staked the animal out on a patch of gramma grass, trying to disregard the unpleasant tingling between his shoulder-blades where a bullet could be expected to strike as he bent down and filtered water through the corner of his scarf into his canteen. The water was warm, sharply alkaline, but welcome none the less for that. He was refilling his canteen when a voice said, "Turn around, feller, an' put yore mitts up."

Rawhide obeyed, there was a short pause and the voice said, "Huh, reckon you're hones'. Ever been in jail?"

"Yeah — once."

"Awright. You could still be hones'. You kin take yore paws down."

Rawhide got to his feet and watched while a man emerged slowly from a mesquite thicket. He was old, battered, and wearing greasy buckskin, but he carried no rifle. "Ben Simmonds," he introduced himself.

"Storm — Rawhide Storm."

"Glad to know you. Eat?"

"Shore could do with it. I ain't got no chuck."

"Then what in tarnation you doin'

on th' Journada?"

"Lookin' for a man."

"Big feller, blonde, ridin' a big black hawss?"

"Could be. He been thisaway?"

"Yeah, thievin' bastard! He took my rifle — my ol' Hawkins. It'll maybe thrun away — dang him, for he won't never make it across."

"No?"

"Course he won't! Fool, that's what he is. Was some mussed up 'bout th' face."

"That's Saxby."

"If you're aimin' to git him — you won't. Me, I don' reckon he'll ever make it across to Pah-Ute hill!" The old man jerked his thumb at the darkening bulk of a mountain that, in the clear desert air, seemed to loom right over them from the westward. He went on getting the meal, slicing more bacon into the pan and mixing dough for biscuits which he slapped on hot stones to cook.

"You aimin' to foller him?" he asked Rawhide.

Rawhide rolled a cigarette and passed over his tobacco sack. "Yeah. You goin' west?"

"Figger to, me an' Joshua an' Jezebel, couple th' best dang mules as ever was foaled." He whistled shrilly and a couple of burros emerged from behind some greasewood, ambled up to the fire and delicately accepted scraps of bacon from their master.

"Kin git by on next to no food, them two — pick a livin' offen th' sand purty near, an' hev to on th' Journada."

"You done it afore?"

"Yeah, been across twice — once each way. This here'll be my third, an' last. If I don' strike it rich down in Sonora this time I'm gonna give up prospectin'."

Rawhide chuckled. "How many times you said that afore, Dad?"

Ben laughed rustily. "Gawd knows — but plenty. This time I mean it. I been friz to death up in Montany, near crazed with heat down in Arizony, an' never yet made much more than a grub stake. But this time I've gotta feelin' I'm gonna strike it rich. Good prospectin' country round here too. Lost Dutchman mine ain't so far."

Ben had been putting food into his mouth all the while he'd been talking, the two mules standing still as statues behind him. "Yeah," he went on reflectively as he picked his teeth with a knife point, "I reckon that when th' good Lawd had jus' about finished this li'l ol' world there were some brickbats o' mountains an' shavin's o'vegetation an' an all-fired sight o' sand an' mortar left over that he didn't 'xactly know what to do with so he jus' dumped it all of a heap-promiskerous, an' it were right here he dumped it." His old eyes became suddenly keen as they probed Rawhide's face.

"What you figgerin' to do, son?" the old man demanded. "You ain't fixed to cross th' Journada — you ain't got no food for one thing."

"I'm lookin' for a man," Rawhide reminded him.

"Yeah, maybe you are, but you needn't pay no more'tention to him — th' desert'll do yore work for you."

"I'm aimin' to do my own work."

Ben shrugged. "Awright. Want to trail along with me?"

"Be glad to — an' grateful. But hev you got enough food for two?"

"Should stretch out. If I had me a shotgun I'd get us plenty o' quail at Marl Springs."

"I got me a rifle — Hawkins single shot. You're welcome to it."

"Right nice o' you — an' thanks. We oughta git by."

"Seen a Conestoga with a man, wife an' daughter? Left Mountain City 'fore I did."

"I ain't seen 'em, but there's another trail from Mountain City. We'll git some sleep now an' start afore dawn. We got quite a step to do tomorrow — forty mile to th' next water."

Only a short while after the sun set

it grew cold, so cold Rawhide was glad of his saddle blankets and the heat of the fire on his feet. The old prospector woke him long before dawn, cooked their breakfast and made preparations with practised speed. Before the sun rose they had made nearly ten miles towards the mountains, which still looked just as far distant. With the sun came swift, fierce heat that reduced them to a dull, miserable acceptance of slow torture. Years in the desert had given Ben Simmonds the capacity so to withdraw into himself as to appear almost in a trance. His riding burro, Joshua, trotted doggedly forward across the sand, the pack burro, Jezebel, followed behind without a leading rope. Rawhide's horse kept up pretty well, but the going was far from suitable for him.

No word was spoken for hour after hour, not even when, at each hour, Ben stopped and wiped the mouths of the three animals with a cloth dampened from his canteen. Both he and Rawhide drank sparingly themselves.

It must have been two or three hours after noon, when they were labouring through a particularly bad stretch of trail where the loose, shifting dust came up over the mules' fetlocks, that old Ben grinned and lifted his head.

"You say there was a waggin ahead of us?" he queried hoarsely.

Rawhide had to clear his parched throat before he could croak, "Yeah, I did. Forans. Three of 'em. Why?"

"They ain't so fur ahead now," Ben told him, and pointed.

Rawhide looked, strained his sun-tired eyes, but couldn't see anything.

"Looks to me though they're in trouble," Ben added.

"Can't even see 'em' leave alone tell if they're stalled."

"Bogged down," Ben went on. "Sand gits worse that-away. Figger we oughta help 'em?"

"Help 'em? Course! Wouldn't you?"

"Son, I dunno. I'm gettin' old, an' helpin' tenderfeet ain't never been nothin' but a fool's game. We're short o' water now. If they're plumb out o' it our li'l drop ain't gonna help any — an' we'll have none."

"Wa'al, I'm for helpin' 'em," Rawhide told him. "You suit yoreself."

Ben shrugged. "Aw, I'm trailin'," he said. "Just figgered to see how you felt. Darter pretty?"

"Mind yore own dang business," Rawhide snapped, still annoyed at the old man's attitude over helping the Forans.

"Don' git steamed up, son," Ben replied mildly. "On'y makes you a dang sight thirstier."

Rawhide's annoyance cooled as quickly as it had risen. He reckoned Ben had been right according to his rights. He had to restrain himself from pushing his tired horse any faster and they plodded on with dogged slowness towards the speck which had at last become visible to Rawhide.

An hour passed before he could see they were indeed in trouble. The

Conestoga had tilted on its way down a rocky dry wash, and lay half on its side partway down the slope, leaving a spilt trail of contents behind it. The mule team had been unharnessed and stood a little distance away, their heads drooping with weariness and panting in the heat which, down in the hollow, was that of a baker's oven.

Until they were quite close to the wagon Rawhide could see no sign of life, although the very fact the mules had been unharnessed meant that someone had survived the accident. Not until his horse blew wearily as he swung out of the saddle was there any movement, and then Marcia's pale, anxious face peered out over the wagon's tilted tailboard.

"Get under cover!" she called urgently. "Hide, Storm! Hide! There's a feller with a rifle around!"

Rawhide stiffened, came to a stop and looked slowly round at the desolate waste of sand and rocks and cactus. Ben turned his quid of tobacco and spat explosively at a lizard that had left its retirement too late. He shifted his Hawkins to the crook of one arm.

"There ain't nobody around here," he said after a long, silent pause.

"But there was," Marcia told him doubtfully. "He shot Dad."

"Shot yore Pa?" Rawhide queried, as he strode towards the stranded wagon. "Killed him?" He hooked his fingers up over the tailboard and pulled himself up to look over the inside. It looked as though an avalanche had hit it, airtights, stores, bedding, cooking utensils — an incredible raffle of gear had drifted to one side as the vehicle tilted. Foran lay on an uneven pile of bedding, a red stain spreading over a rough bandage covering the upper part of his right arm. Mrs. Foran lay on a lopsided bunk, her face waxen.

Rawhide let himself down, then looked into the girl's pale, strained face. The barely controlled terror in her eyes brought a pang to his heart. He reached up one hand and gently stroked her cheek. "Don' look like yore pa's hurt bad," he said. "What's th' matter with yore ma?"

"She — she tried to get the gun away and he struck her, an old woman!"

Rawhide glanced at Ben. "Same feller — Saxby. Big, blonde, face mussed up?"

Marcia added.

"I should ha' killed him when I had the chance."

"Would ha' saved me my rifle," Ben said sourly. "Gimme a hand up, Rawhide. I seen a fair few gunshot wounds."

"Careful o' th' waggin, it could tilt further. You better come down, Marcia." He helped her down and held her in his arms, her face lifting naturally to his as his arms tightened round her and their lips met briefly.

Then she pushed him away. "He came on us suddenly," she said. "Told us he had to have food and water. We — we would have helped him, but he put his rifle on Dad and threatened him, so Dad said we'd none to spare. Then he shot Dad. He said Dad tried to pull a gun, but Dad hasn't got one. Then Ma went for him an' he hit her, the mules bolted — an' here we are." She broke down, sobbing, in Rawhide's arms.

"An' you got 'em both up in th' waggin an' staked out th' mules," he said.

"Yeah, I — I managed it; they aren't very heavy."

"This feller — this Saxby, he take food an' water?"

"He took some food — an' water. He spilled what he couldn't take — there's hardly any left in the barrel."

"What I tell you?" Ben growled from inside. "No water! An' this feller needs some. He ain't hurt bad, but he'll git a fever soon. He's got fifteen miles an' a long pull up to Marl Springs. Hell!" The old man made a swallowing sort of grunt and Rawhide grinned as he realised how nearly Ben had squirted tobacco juice over the inside of the wagon.

"How's th' ol' woman?"

"I'm better, young feller. An' I ain't so old," Mrs. Foran said, her voice shaky but quite determined. "I reckon I owe you an apology," she said. "I bawled you out, said killin' was wicked. It ain't! It's too good for a man that'll spill water in th' desert an' leave a wounded man an' two women thirsty! If you find him, young feller, you got my permission to shoot him!"

"Be glad to, ma'am," Rawhide replied. "But right now we better git movin'."

"Move? How can we move? Th' wagon must be smashed!"

"Reckon not, ma'am. Conestoga's built for this sort o' work, an' I picked out a tough 'un. I'll go see." Rawhide kissed Marcia again; this time the answering pressure of her lips was warmer, but she whispered, "Don't let Ma see you. She chased off th' last feller with a hatchet!"

Rawhide smiled at her, went round the wagon and found to his relief that the stout, seasoned wood frame, axles and wheels had suffered no serious damage.

Ben clambered down from the vehicle, looked sourly at Rawhide and said, "Awright?"

"Yeah. Bent up a bit, but not to matter."

Ben spat reflectively on a flat rock. "Shore is hot," he stated, then he stared away up at Pah Ute Mountain.

"Kin we make it?" Rawhide asked.

"Dunno. But we ain't gonna make it by no rushin' around. There's a couple o' picks in my pack saddle on Jezebel. We'll hev to dig this dang thing level; if we pull it out we could bust somethin' — which wouldn't be so good."

Rawhide moved over to him and tapped his canteen. It was empty.

"You give it to Foran?"

"Mine to give, wasn't it?" Ben demanded.

"Guess who you ain't kiddin'," Rawhide

178

replied quietly. "Here, Marcia, there's a little in here. You an' yore ma drink it — slow."

"But you'll need it if you're gonna dig."

Ben slanted one eye up at the sun. "We'll all need it," he said soberly.

Rawhide had been hot before, but out on the open desert there had been at least a suspicion of a breeze to mitigate the fierce heat. Down in the dry wash there was not the faintest breath of air. The heat was a foretaste of inferno, the sun blazing down so that the heat blasted back up from the rocks; rocks which burnt at the touch of flesh, rocks so hot they would have fried an egg in an instant.

Before ten minutes had passed a trip hammer beat at the base of Rawhide's head, a mottled mist danced before his eyes as he wielded his heavy pick; no more sweat ran from his parched body, his tongue felt like a thick strip of felt, dust coated from the choking clouds raised by their labour. Old

Ben worked steadily, apparently slowly but the stones moved easily under the cunning blows from his pick. He seemed unaffected by the heat and didn't bother to remove his ragged, sweat-stained buck-skin vest. In half an hour's fierce labour they succeeded in picking out the rocks from under the raised side of the wagon so that it slowly settled back more or less to a level keel. Rawhide leant on his pick, his brain numb, conscious only of an overpowering desire to drink, to plunge his head in the cool depths of a sparkling stream — the stream he could see only a few yards away.

"Easy, feller, easy." Ben's warning voice brought him back to reality. "Easy — it ain't but false water. We got more work yet."

Rawhide's brain absorbed the words only slowly. He moved his thick tongue experimentally and managed to croak, "More work?"

"Yeah. We gotta clear a path for th' waggin, pull it up outa this dry wash or it may overset again an' we wouldn't want that. Dunno why'n hell they ever drove down into this dang wash."

"We thought maybe there would be some shade," Marcia told them apologetically.

Ben spat viciously. "There ain't no shade on th' Journada," he growled. "C'mon, Rawhide, let's clear these dang rocks."

It took another half-hour's work to clear an even partway smooth route up out of the dry wash, and at the end of that time Rawhide was barely conscious. He had to be forcibly prevented from heading away into the desert towards the stream he could then see more clearly than anything else. A couple of sips of water and a few minutes' rest in the comparative shade under the Conestoga went a little way towards restoring his sanity, and he hitched up the mules without much trouble.

"I better drive," Ben said, and clambered up on the seat. "Bring them dang mules o' mine, feller, they don' need to be dragged neither."

Rawhide staggered to his horse, hauled himself into the saddle and sat there slackly flogging his brain to think out what he had to do next. Working almost entirely by instinct, he gathered the reins of Ben's mules, kneed his mount and got the animal on the move. The horse hadn't gone a couple of yards before the burros' reins jerked out of his hands — the mules had decided they didn't want to move. Scarlet anger flared for a moment in Rawhide's brain, his hand went to his gun butt, but it faded as abruptly, leaving only an empty hopelessness in its place.

"Hey, Ben!" he croaked. "These dang jarheads is balky!"

But Ben didn't hear; he'd got the Conestoga on the move, and the noise it made drowned out Rawhide's call. Rawhide swore helplessly as he saw the wagon roll, lurching up out of the dry wash. Suddenly he felt terribly alone, unpleasantly aware of the immensity of the desert and its overwhelming power to engulf him, reduce him to a heap of sun-bleached bones. He turned slowly in his saddle, angry because of the dent that had been made in his self-respect. He didn't like being self-sufficient, yet when a couple of balky mules hadn't moved the instant he wanted them to he had bleated for help like a kid with toothache.

"Take a pull at yoreself, Storm," he mumbled. "Ain't no dang desert gonna git you down!"

He dismounted, retrieved the mule reins and lashed them together before he dallied them over his own saddle horn. "There, you dang, stupid, obstinit bastards!" he croaked at them. "See if you kin pull again a hawss!" They could — and they did quite easily. The horse was completely incapable of budging them until Rawhide pulled a gun and shot at Joshua's rear heels, blasting pebbles out from under them. After that the mules followed on as docile as oxen. When his horse at last managed the grade up out of the dry wash, Rawhide was surprised to see how far ahead the wagon had gone. Already the dust cloud it raised was faint and unreal in the heat. In fact, the 'false water' was once again floating before his eyes, and appeared more substantial.

"I ain't fallin' for that agin," he told himself, "nor I ain't goin' crazy — I been near it once an' that's enough. Git movin, Storm, an' quit pikin'." He held himself rigidly under control as he rode on, not trying to urge his horse, not thinking about the thirst that tortured him, not thinking even about Saxby, whose fault it was that he was there at all. He just rode, sitting slackly in the saddle, his eyes as closed as his mind, trying to school himself to the capacity for patient endurance as in old Ben Simmonds. Gradually he overhauled the wagon and came up with it as the tired mules started to haul it up the slope of Pah Ute Mountain. Ben dozed on the seat, but managed to raise a languid hand as Rawhide drew alongside.

"You hev trouble with them mules?" the old man asked.

"Yeah — some," Rawhide admitted hoarsely.

"Be some more soon," Ben said. "We'll need to hitch 'em on this lot an' they ain't gonna like it. We shan't git up else, though."

Already the six-mule team was labouring, and after a glance up at the grade they had to climb, Rawhide agreed — but silently, for it was difficult for him to talk. Marcia put her head round the tilt and smiled at him.

"Dad's conscious," she told him, "an' plumb grateful again to both o' you." She kissed Ben's left ear lightly and the man's face turned an even deeper shade of red.

"I ain't gonna marry yer," he grunted. "I got three wives awready, an' any one o' them'd be too many. C'mon, Rawhide, let's git them mules hitched." He stopped his own team, slammed on the wagon brake and climbed from the seat, as chipper as a ten-year-old, then took the mules' reins from Rawhide's saddle.

"Now, you two gopher-headed no-goods," he croaked at them, "you're gonna do some work for once in yore useless lives. Giddap there!" He led them to the head of the team, but Joshua evidently guessed what was in the old man's mind, for he lashed out with his near side hoof, a kick that would have crippled Ben if he hadn't jumped out of the way. Ben cursed the mule heartily, fetched him one in the ribs. "Figgered I was gettin' old — huh? Jus' for that you'll pull double. Marcia, gimme that coil o' rope I seen under th' seat, will you?"

The girl threw down the rope and in a very few minutes Ben had lashed his two beasts to the wagon tongue. Then he lifted Jezebel's packs from her saddle and slung them into the back of the wagon. "Ain't no reason for you to work double tides, gal," he told her, as he got back on the seat. "Giddap!" he called, cracking the whip behind Joshua's left ear — "Giddap, you misbegotten son of a coyote an' a cactus!"

The wagon creaked into motion and crept on up the slope. Inside, Foran began muttering, his voice rising gradually to a high pitch of delirium, a rusty, thirst-roughened voice that died away as his wife soothed him. Marcia looked once out of the back of the tilt and managed a sort of smile at Rawhide, then the swirling just hid her as the wagon wheel lurched into a hollow. Rawhide relapsed once more into a semi-coma as his horse reluctantly followed the wagon. An hour passed — two hours — an eternity. He had no idea of time, time no longer meant anything; thirst bounded his whole consciousness, thirst and the mirages thirst brought. He saw long, cool steins of beer, snowy slopes of mountains, willow thickets beside crystal streams, the slap and gurgle of a full bucket emerging from a well, anything rather than the ever-present agony of a tongue that filled his whole mouth. He was only dimly aware that the trail in front of him no longer rose but had pitched over on to the level and that he had overtaken the wagon. Ben's croaked words brought him back to reality: "That there's Marl Springs."

Rawhide blinked his sun-strained eyes and saw, half a mile away, a patch of stunted mesquite. Then he saw the puff of smoke from the rifle that sent a bullet sighing over his head.

9

AUTOMATICALLY, Rawhide released his grip on his horse, and the nearly exhausted animal stopped at once as the sharp crack of the hidden rifleman's second shot came flatly across the rough desert. Rawhide tried, again automatically, to open his dust-caked mouth to say, "Saxby," but no sound — only a throaty rasp — came from his arid throat. Ben had pulled the wagon to a stop; he looked wearily across at Rawhide and went through the motions of spitting without success.

"Same feller," he grunted. "Leastwise I guess it is. Don' look so good shuttin' us off from water."

Anger burned like a fire in Rawhide's brain; he would have been incapable of words even if he had been able to speak. He kneed his horse over to the wagon and held out his hand; he didn't have to speak. Ben gave him the Hawkins and a handful of cartridges; he glanced once into Marcia's fear-stricken eyes, then urged his horse on as he replaced the cartridge in the breech of the old single-shot rifle. Another shot came from the Springs and whined past his ear before he had gone fifty yards; he threw his rifle to his shoulder and fired at the puff of smoke before it had dispersed, blinking as the powder blast came back up into his face, through the ill-fitting breech of his badly fouled weapon, telling him that each shot he fired carried the risk of the rifle bursting; however, he was too blazing with anger to be deterred by such a risk and fired again and again, his face soon black from blow-back, his eyes smarting from the sting of the powder.

More shots came back at him; one nicked his horse and made the animal buck-jump weary though it was — almost unseating Rawhide.

He swore mentally, all the angrier because he couldn't curse out loud, then the hidden rifle fired again, but with a difference, the report not being sharp at all but dull and lasting longer. "Earthed his gun," Rawhide's brain told him hopefully. "I must ha' shot close an' got him rattled."

At the Springs a man rose from cover and raced for another mesquite clump behind which Rawhide saw a horse — his horse Dancer; Saxby limped as he ran, limped badly but with a desperate urgency. "No Colt," Rawhide remembered. "I took it offa him at Mountain City." He lifted the Hawkins and fired at the figure struggling through the sand, but the worn rifling of the barrel let him down. He knew he had missed from the way the muzzle kicked off target.

Saxby reached his horse, scrambled into the saddle and jumped it into a dead run away into the almost level rays of the setting sun. Rawhide lowered his Hawkins, and suddenly found he was trembling violently, trembling he found he was completely unable to check as his mount stumbled on towards the water it had scented. Ben released the wagon brake and the mules also managed a shambling sort of trot that brought them to the Springs before Rawhide. When at last he slid wearily out of the saddle, stood on his unsteady legs and looked round him he was appalled. Springs? How, his tired brain wondered, could these two muddy holes in the ground, surrounded by stunted mesquite and cactus, be described as Springs? He turned to face Ben as the wagon creaked to a stop.

"Springs?" he croaked. "Springs? I seen more water in a puddle in a bar!"

Ben fixed the brake and got down from the wagon, his hands at the small of his back as he eased his ancient muscles.

"It ain't good," he admitted, "but there's water here. That feller lit out right smart?" He nodded towards the west where the cloud of dust raised by Saxby's horse was already fading from sight.

"Sanded his rifle," Rawhide explained. "Sounded like it bust. How'd we git water?"

Ben grunted and walked stiffly round to the back of the wagon, fetched out his pack saddles, unleashing one with maddening slowness. "How'd we git it?" Rawhide croaked urgently,. "Them wimmen is thirsty!"

"Me too — an' you, I guess," Ben said, producing a canvas bucket and a rope. "Here's how we git it." He groaned as he heaved himself to his feet, lurched across to a ruined and muddy hole in the ground down which he lowered the bucket on the end of the rope. He let it lie for a while, then pulled it up full of the muddiest, most evil-smelling water Rawhide had ever seen, but it tasted wonderful all the same. They didn't even wait for it to clear — as Ben had said it would — but each drank just enough to take the

193

edge off their raging thirsts. Foran was unconscious, and Marcia dampened a piece of cloth, wiped his lips and dribbled a little down his throat. Ben climbed up into the wagon to look at the sick man, shook his head privately at Rawhide when he came back down again. He pulled Rawhide aside.

"He ain't gonna last long, I figger," he whispered. "Gone that sort o' grey colour."

"On'y one bullet hit, huh?"

"Yeah. But that Hawkins o' mine throws a big slug, smashed his arm up considerable, an' he's lost a lot o' blood. Heat an' thirst don' help none. You figger we'll have more trouble with that jasper?"

Rawhide shrugged — "Dunno," he said, "not till I see whether his rifle did bust; I didn't see him carry it away." He searched around the clump which had provided Saxby with cover, soon found the rifle — and a patch of blood — "I creased him," he muttered. "Made him jump. Rifle must ha' fell outa his hand an' sanded; he didn't know, an' th' next shell bust it. No," he told Ben as he rejoined the old man, "he won't bother us no more, rifle did bust like I figgered."

"Awright then, we kin have us a fire," Ben grunted. "You git us some more water drawed — there's a tin bucket in th' wagon, use mine for a filter an' then we shan't be eatin' more than half th' range; there's two water holes but you kin on'y git about two buckets an hour from each, after that we gotta wait for 'em to fill up. Lookit them dang mules!" The mules, as thirsty as their master, were milling round the wells, treading more mud into the already near-choked holes. Rawhide had to beat them away, then beat the others away as he watered each in turn. There was grass of sorts, thin, wiry, unsucculent looking stuff but the mules were so hungry they even chewed dusty mesquite leaves.

By the time Rawhide had watered the stock Ben had a fire going and a meal nearly cooked; they ate hungrily, wordlessly, the shadow of Foran's condition hanging over them.

As Marcia finished her second cup of black, bitter coffee she looked at Rawhide.

"That man — you knew him?"

"Yeah, I knew him," Rawhide said curtly, and then, influenced perhaps by the incredibly brilliant array of stars spread overhead that seemed almost close enough to touch, he spoke more freely than he had ever spoken before. "Yeah," he went on, "I know him. He ran off with my wife an' framed me for murder. Three days ago he killed my wife — murdered her because she hadn't got no more dinero to give him. Saxby ain't a nice feller — not none at all."

"You think we'll be able to catch him?"

"Maybe not."

"But th' Journada will," Ben stated flatly. "Th' Journada'll ketch him an' turn him mad with heat an' thirst an' flies, he'll die an' he won't die pleasant. You kin be dang good an' shore o' that, Miss Marcia."

At his words a silence fell upon the small circle round the camp, and presently Mrs. Foran got up and went to the wagon to resume her watch over her husband. Ben busied himself with the camp chores, and drawing more water.

"You miss yore wife?" Marcia asked quietly.

"Miss her? Not any. I did at first, on account I'd gotten so used to havin' her around. But now — hell, no! Though I wouldn't ha' wanted her to die th' way she did. Why'd you ask?"

"Me? Oh, I just wondered. I — I guess I better go an' see how Dad is." She went away hurriedly, but not before Rawhide had had time to see the flush that darkened her face.

"Nice gal, ain't she?" Ben asked, spitting into the fire and making it hiss.

"Yeah — some. You reckon we

oughta watch out for this feller?"

"He ain't got no gun!"

"No, but we hev. Could be he'll try to sneak up an' try to git one o' ours."

"Lit out like he didn't figger to come back."

"Yeah, but . . . "

"Hell, ain't nobody gonna sneak up on us while them mules o' mine are around, either one o' them'll give us plenty warning."

"Awright, guess we'll sleep then. We shore need it."

They woke in the morning to find that Foran was dead; the shock of the heavy bullet, even though it hit no vital part, had been too much for his small reserve of strength, coming as it did after long weeks of strain; loss of blood and the fierce heat of the Journada had done the rest. Rawhide and Ben scratched out a shallow grave, piled earth and stones over the little man's body before the first buzzard came sailing down out of the dawn sky. Dry-eyed, Marcia and her mother watched, and afterwards made a brave pretence of eating breakfast.

"What you figger to do, Miz Foran?" Rawhide asked her gently. "Me an' Ben we'll see you on yore way back — if that's what you want."

"We don't want. Me and Marcia, we've talked it over some, an' we're goin' on — that's if you don' mind us comin' with you. We wouldn't want to go back to Ohio 'thout Dad — ain't nothin' for us there. We reckon to take our chance in Californy. Dad — wa'al, it was my fault we ever come west, so havin' started it I reckon we oughta finish it — for Dad's sake."

"Suits us," Rawhide replied. "Reckon we'll travel all th' easier for havin' a waggin' along."

Ben spat with more than usual force. "Suits me," he grunted. "An' now we better git goin', we gotta a long ways to travel."

"How far's th' next water, Ben?"

"Ute Springs — 'bout forty mile, an'

mighty poor travellin' — all loose sand an 'some stretches o' dang nasty rocks thrown in for variety."

"Uhuh. An' these Ute Springs — they th' same as these?"

"Naw. Bes' water on' th' Journada. Kin git a bathe there if you want."

"A bathe? You mean there's enough water to swim in?"

"Wa'al, not to swim, but purty near."

Marcia picked at her stained, sweat-streaked clothes. "That would be just wonderful," she said. "Too good to be true."

"It ain't true yet," Ben told her grumpily. "We ain't even started. We should be five miles away 'stead o' yammerin' here!"

Five minutes sufficed to pack up the camp, hitch the mules and get on the move; neither Mrs. Foran nor Marcia looked round at the little pile of stones that covered Foran, but it was obvious that it required a tremendous effort on both their parts not to look.

The sun came up over the horizon with a rush as the wagon pulled away from Marl Springs and in a short while the heat was once again searing in its intensity. Rawhide slumped in his saddle and withdrew into himself as much as he could, settling to another day of enduring sweat and thirst, although thirst should not be such a danger that day, for Ben had dredged up enough water to fill a small barranco in the back of the wagon.

* * *

Lost in the desert, crazed, and near dying of thirst, the man was mocked by visions. Fear had sharpened his spurs as he had run his horse from Marl Springs the previous night, fear of Rawhide's vengeance which he had thought to be comfortably out-distanced, fear of vengeance for the stupid cruelty he had shown to the Forans. In some half-crazed superstitious way he connected the bursting of his rifle with Storm.

He didn't regret what he had done — to his warped brain it seemed that he had done nothing wrong; he only regretted that punishment should be treading so closely upon his heels. He had ridden hard for an hour during which a measure of sanity returned to him and he realised the desert was bad and dangerous ground for night riding. If the horse broke a leg . . .

He had stopped, dismounted, turned back to watch the distant spark of light which was the camp fire at Marl Springs. Curses bubbled in his throat as he thought of the food cooking there, he cursed again as he sucked water from his canteen and tightened his belt a notch, for the food he had taken from the Forans was almost done; he bitterly resented the fact that back there at the Springs people he had wronged should be eating round the warmth of a fire while he shivered, hungry out on the desert. It wasn't fair. The man cursed again because he had no rifle and could not Injun up on them to shoot at the easy targets. He rolled himself in his single blanket, slept for the few hours the cold permitted him, then woke chill and shivery, ate a little and rode on — carelessly, so carelessly that when his horse stumbled he was thrown so heavily he was stunned for a minute.

He had inspired only hate in his big black horse, and when he came to himself the horse had gone. His head aching with a blinding ache, he got to his feet and stumbled after the horse, but the tracks soon faded from the wind-winnowed expanse of blazing sand that stretched away as far as he could see in every direction, bounded only by the dim bulk of the Pah Ute hills to the east. To the west the heat haze hid Mosca Mountain; there were long, level stretches where nothing grew, just sand the colour of bleached bones, then there were ridges and hillocks with a scattering of sparse, dry creosote bushes which gave only a mockery of shade. The sun beat down pitilessly and he got the impression that the sun was a mocking fiend wielding a white-hot bar of steel, a crazed demon that beat incessantly with the bar upon his head so that he could feel the impact of every blow, thunderous on his ear-drums.

After an hour the man had lost all sense of direction. He had fallen many times, his hat was gone and the sun blazed full on his head. For a while he lay in the spurious shadow of a warped cactus and, as he lay, he saw the heat haze quiver, dance, and change miraculously into a cool pool fringed by tall willows. He lurched to his feet and ran stumbling forward with a choking cry to hurl himself into the pool, only to pitch his face in the burning sand, eyes, nose and mouth filled with the hot grit; groaning, he rolled over, spitting sand; the vision faded and he knew he was lost, knew he was going to die, to die of heat and thirst, alone, friendless, out in that desert to which his crimes had led him. For a moment — just a moment — he regretted those crimes, but the moment passed and some remnant of the survival urge forced him to his feet.

He went on again, not knowing where, not knowing how, until the mirage once again took possession of his brain and once again cruelly deluded him. That time he lay a long while, for the tenacity to which he clung to life was fading, and it now took longer to spur him to his feet. Once again he staggered on until, again, he was mocked by the vision of a wagon, a wagon that seemed to rise from the sand only to sink again — and vanish. Barely able to stand, his eyes red-rimmed, he watched it go, then he wept the awful agonised weeping of a man who had no tears to moisten his sun-seared eyeballs; he couldn't help but look again and saw, in agony, the eight-mule team drag the wagon over another sand swale. He rushed towards it, his strength galvanically restored by hope, only to see it vanish once more. He whirled, after one tottering moment of indecision, and ran stumbling, falling, staggering up again, plunging out across the waste of sand. He didn't hear the hoofbeats of a horse behind him, didn't feel the steely fingers that turned him over after he had fallen yet again; but sanity returned for one splintered second as he looked up into the pitiless eyes of the one man he least wanted to see.

Rawhide let his limp shoulders flop back on the sand and stood staring down at the man he had good cause to hate; he looked round and saw the whole story in Saxby's crazed tracks. As old Ben had forecast, the desert had claimed Saxby, claimed him only for Rawhide to clutch him back at the eleventh hour.

"Who is it?" Ben's voice startled Rawhide from his train of thought; he looked round to see that Ben had brought the wagon close up on him.

"Saxby," he replied.

"He dead?"

"Not quite." He drew a Colt

deliberately, thumbed back the hammer and lifted the muzzle.

"Rawhide, you can't do that!" Marcia screamed. "It's murder!"

Rawhide slowly let the Colt drop to his side. "He murdered yore dad."

"That — that was different. Dad was on his feet."

"He had no more chance agin Saxby than Saxby has now — your Dad didn't savvy guns. An' anyway, it's better than jus' leavin' him."

"That what you're gonna do?"

"Hell, what else kin we do?"

"Give him water for a start. He's dyin' o' thirst, ain't he?"

Marcia sprang down from the wagon, carried a canteen of water across and knelt by Saxby, who lifted his head and moistened his lips. Soon his eyelids stirred, his lips parted and she trickled a little more water through them; a shudder passed over his body and his hands came up, clawlike, tearing at the canteen. "Gently," she warned as she moved the canteen out of his reach.

Following the water source, Saxby's eyes fell upon Rawhide and the Colt still in his hand. "I'm sick," he croaked. "You can't shoot a dyin' man."

Rawhide shoved the Colt back in its holster. "Wa'al, what now? What you aimin' to do with him?" he demanded harshly.

"Get him well," Marcia replied, as sharply. "An' then hand him over to th' sheriff in th' first town we're comin' to."

"That'll be in Californy," Ben reminded her, "an' there ain't no sheriff gonna be interested in what this jasper done in Colorado."

"I don' care," Marcia stated flatly, 'just ain't possible either to shoot this man or leave him to die — an' I ain't gonna have it happen. Help me carry him to the wagon."

"I ain't havin' that murderin' skunk in back o' me," Mrs. Foran cut in. "Don' you recollect he killed yore dad, gal?"

Anger blazed in Marcia's eyes as she

rose and faced her mother.

"I don't care what he's done — I ain't havin' him left to die!"

Ben looked at Rawhide and shrugged helplessly then got down from his seat. "This feller," he grunted as he lifted Saxby's feet, "is luckier than a whole field o' four-leaved clovers; he should ha' died long since — maybe he's jus' so dang bad that even th' Devil don' want him."

None too gently they carried Saxby to the wagon and lifted him to the bed Foran had occupied. Rawhide went back to his horse; Ben to his driving seat.

"I'm gonna look for his hawss," Rawhide said as he settled himself in the saddle. "Can't be far away — an' he was my hawss once."

"Awright," Ben replied. "Ute Springs are due west o' here. See that notch in them mountains? — that's Mosca Pass, Pass o' th' caves. Aim for that an' you'll hit th' Springs on th' way."

Rawhide watched the Conestoga roll

away hoping, for some unfathomable reason, that Marcia would look out and wave to him; he was unaccountably annoyed when she didn't.

Wind had sifted sand over much of Saxby's crazily tortuous trail and Rawhide worked back largely by guesswork to the place where Saxby had been thrown; from there he tracked Dancer fairly easily, for the horse had got upon a flat shelf of soft sandstone where his steelshod hoofs had left marks. In an hour Rawhide found him, and thereafter by changing off he made better time.

10

BEN hadn't exaggerated over Ute Springs. Water gushing up through a fault in the limestone rock had formed for itself a pool twenty feet wide of water so clear its five-foot depth looked but one; from this pool the icy water flowed out and down through a series of half a dozen other rock pools before vanishing irretrievably into the desert sand. Mesquite, willows, and a few stunted live oaks somehow found a living in the sparse but moist soil; there was shade, wood for firing, even some coarse bunch grass for the animals.

Even by changing off Rawhide had been unable to make up all the time he had lost in trailing Dancer, and darkness was falling as he reached the camp; but for the fire Ben had lit he might easily have passed the

Springs. As it was, the sight of the fire, the tethered mules, the parked wagon and the smell of bacon to some extent lifted the black cloud of anger that had settled over him; he tried to decide whether or not he would have pulled the trigger when Saxby lay helpless under his Colt, and it infuriated him that he couldn't be sure, couldn't even be sure of what he would do if he were again presented with the same opportunity. If Marcia hadn't been there — that perhaps was the root of his anger, that he should have allowed a slip of a girl to come between him and Saxby's death.

Now, as he rode into camp, black anger welled up again as he saw Saxby sitting with his back against a wagon wheel, with a plate on his knees; a Saxby changed almost beyond recognition from the wreck of a man he had been hours before; he was still emaciated — yes, but clean, washed and shaved, a Saxby whose eyes met Rawhide's boldly as he swung out of the saddle and who had the infernal gall to say cheerfully, "Hi, feller! Guess I gotta thank you twice, one for findin' me an' one for findin' my hawss!"

Rawhide could only stare, fury choking his throat; he turned away, wordless, unsaddled and watered both horses before he drank himself, sluicing his face and neck in the wonderful coolness of the water. Then, and only then, did he return to the circle of light round the fire.

"It ain't yore hawss," he said. "I bought him in Mountain City."

"Then o' course you got a bill o' sale for him?"

Rawhide clamped his teeth on wicked words, words he couldn't speak while Marcia and her mother were there.

"I ain't," he said at last, his voice thick with rage, his hand quivering over a gun butt. "Nor you ain't neither — you thievin', murderin' bastard!"

"Them ain't words you oughta use to a feller whose life you saved," Saxby replied mildly, with a sanctimonious 'but I forgive you' expression on his face. "I'm plumb grateful, but right now I ain't in a position to resent them words personal."

Rawhide shrugged, helpless with fury; he looked at Ben, who crouched by the fire, all his attention centred on a skillet he was holding. "He nuts?" he queried.

"Says he ain't Saxby, says his name's Smith," Ben growled.

"But you . . . " Rawhide swung round to Marcia, "you know he's th' feller that shot yore dad?"

Marcia flushed. "I — I — we ain't shore; that man had a beard, had his hat pulled low."

"Gawd gimme strength," Rawhide pleaded. "This here's Saxby, used to punch cows for me; I'd know him anywhere!"

Then Saxby smiled at him again, a maddening superior smile. "I know how it is, feller," he said. "Why earlier today I wouldn't ha' known my own ma! You musta had a touch o' th' sun, feller."

He had his nerve with him, did Saxby — he must have known by the glare in Rawhide's eyes just how near death he was, but he kept a secret sort of smile on his face. Rawhide's eyes shuttled to Ben. "You, Ben, he took yore rifle! You reckernise him?"

Ben shook his head slowly. "Ain't shore," he said regretfully. "Light weren't so good an' I ain't certain. Feller that took my Hawkins had a beard, this feller ain't got no beard nor he ain't got no rifle."

Rawhide swung back to Saxby and stared at him, beginning almost to doubt himself whether it was Saxby. The clean-shaven face showed no signs of the damage Rawhide's fists had done to Saxby back in Mountain City, but the bruises could have cleared in the interval.

"You're Saxby," he said, "an' I know it — I'll prove it too! I'm gonna watch you like a hawk, feller, so don' think you're gonna git away with nothin'!"

Saxby still smiled and turned towards

Marcia with a tiny shrug of his shoulders which said clearly as if he had put it into words, 'Pore feller's got a touch o' th' sun, but me — I'm big-hearted, he saved my life so I ain't gonna resent nothin'.' Saxby was still clearly suffering from the effects of his narrow escape from death, but even so Rawhide understood only too easily how he had taken in Alin, for both Marcia and her mother appeared to have completely lost their suspicions of him.

Rawhide swallowed his fury, got his food from Ben and ate ravenously, as he ate he tried to get used to the idea that for the rest of the Journada he would have to travel with Saxby — unless he went off on his own. He wasn't anxious to do that, for he had already seen enough of the Journada to know that without Ben's experience he'd have little chance of getting through, and anyway he wanted to watch Saxby — he watched him then, talking away to Marcia as easily as if they'd been sitting in her mother's parlour back in Ohio.

Rawhide found the food turned sour in his mouth as he watched Saxby smile and smirk and pay subtle little compliments such as Rawhide could no more have got his tongue around than fly. He bolted his food, sluiced the crocks in the pool before he built a cigarette, lit it and smoked savagely.

Ben ambled across, lowered himself to the ground and spat into the fire. "Hell of a help you were," Rawhide told the old man bitterly.

"When I said I weren't shore — I weren't. I on'y seen him once, remember," Ben spoke defensively. "An' them wimmen they shore fell for him, worked hard at him in th' waggin an' all."

"Wa'al, I am shore, an' I've a dang good mind to . . . "

"To what, Rawhide? You can't jus' up an' shoot him now."

"Not jus' like that maybe — but there is a way!" He got swiftly to his feet and walked across to the wagon. Saxby still sat with his back against a wheel, his face lifted to the stars, his eyes upon Marcia who sat on a case of airtights, a shawl round her shoulders, for the night was already chill.

"Denver ain't nothin'," Saxby was saying in a pleasant, easy voice. "Why, it ain't hardly anythin' but a frontier town still — on'y a few years ago they had an Apache scare there. Chicago — that's more of a town, but Chicago ain't got nothin' compared with N'York. There's a place for you — theatres, hotels where they got carpets up aroun' yore ankles, restaurants where you kin git th' dandiest food — quail'n all sorts . . . " Then he saw Rawhide and twisted round to grin up at him. "Hi, feller!" he said. "Come to 'pologise?"

Rawhide's right hand bunched, but drew back automatically. Only by an effort did he prevent himself from smashing into Saxby's face.

"Apologise, hell!" he growled, his

ungraciousness accentuated by his awareness of being ungracious. "I'm callin' you th' same as I did afore — a murderin', thievin' coyote! Here's yore time to resent it!" He drew one Colt, broke it and offered it to Saxby. "Git up on yore legs, polecat! An' you kin git an even break!"

"Rawhide!" Marcia burst out. "You ain't gonna fight?"

"I mean to. This is Saxby — I been fixin' to salivate him for quite some time. I missed out on one chance, but I ain't doin' that again."

Saxby put on an expression of the utmost bewilderment. "But what for should you an' me tangle? I'm grateful to you, plumb grateful, but . . ."

"Aw, quit yore palaverin', Saxby. Take this iron!"

"But I ain't Saxby — my name's Smith!"

"Yeah? An' I'm Benedict Arnold. Quit yammerin', Saxby, this is th' end o' th' road for you."

"Storm, are you gone crazy?" Mrs.

Foran demanded. She had been doing something in the wagon and now came to the tilt, glared down at Rawhide. "That feller says he didn't have anythin' to do with killin' Pa, an' I'm believin' him. That feller had a plumb mean, vicious face — th' which same Smith ain't."

"You shut yore yap!" Rawhide bawled at her, too furious by then to think clearly. "Keep outa this — it ain't no woman's quarrel."

Marcia moved in a flash from her cracker box, snatched the Colt from Rawhide's hand, snapped it to and pointed it at him. "We'll have no killin' here," she said, her voice as shaky as the heavy revolver. "I reckon Ma's right an' you've gone nuts, Rawhide. We can't prove this man is who you say he is, an' . . . "

Rawhide shrugged helplessly, took the gun from her easily enough and turned away. As he went he heard Saxby say, "Them restaurants in Noo York, Miss Foran, they really are somethin' — all glass an' mirrors, an' . . . " His soft voice became inaudible as Rawhide slouched back to sit beside Ben.

"He shore has got them wimmen buffaloed," the old prospector said. "Charm a monkey off a stick, he would."

Rawhide grunted. His brain — now cleared of fury — was busy with a problem; he rolled and smoked half a dozen cigarettes before the glimmering of an idea came to him. 'When yore up against a feller,' his father had been used to tell him, 'go for him where he's weakest; if he can't take a punch on th' chin hit him there; if he ain't no good with a rifle keep him outa short gun range.' "Yeah, an' Saxby drinks," Rawhide reminded himself. Then out loud he asked, "Any whisky in that wagon?"

Ben spat contemptuously. "She's again it; I had me a small snort outa th' jug I had in my pack saddle an' she purty near burnt th' skin off th' back o' my neck, said it was pizen, an' hell an' damnation an' I dunno what all else."

"You got any left?"

"On'y 'bout a quart, ain't hardly more'n a couple o' swallers — good cornjuice too. Want some?"

"Yeah, but not for us — him."

"That jasper? Feller you figger done all what you said? Miz Foran's plumb correct — you are crazy!"

"I ain't. I gotta idea that'll make him open up."

"Uhuh. You figger to make him open up by havin' him drink my good corn likker?"

"Yeah, that's th' idea."

"Wa'al I figger not. If he is th' coyote you think I wouldn't wanta waste my likker on him."

"Aw, look Ben, I'll buy it offa you."

The old man scratched his stubbly chin. "Wa'al, dunno as I'd sell it to you, dinero ain't no use out here on th' Journada — an' whisky we could need. Still, I could do with a snort my ownself." Still muttering, he got up, went over to his pack and came back with a stoppered jug. "I ain't likin' this," he grumbled, as he set it down carefully between them.

"Nor's Saxby," Rawhide said. "He's seen it an' he's lickin' his lips. Me an' you, we gotta drink small, ol' timer. Easy!" he warned, as Ben unstoppered the jug, swung it to his lips and took a gulp that made his eyes water.

Ben swung the jug down, belched, wiped his straggly moustache with the back of his hand and belched again. "Try it," he invited.

Rawhide took a cautious mouthful, making it look as though he took a lot, watching Saxby as he put the jug down. "Right smooth likker," he commented.

Saxby moved as if to ease cramped muscles, then slowly got up, said something to Marcia before walking round the fire to stand over Ben and Rawhide.

"Wouldn't be likker you got there,

gents?" he asked softly.

Rawhide looked up at him. "An' if it is?"

"If it is I could shore use a slug. Ain't had a drink in a coon's age."

It cost Rawhide an effort to be civil even with the end he had in view, but he managed it after a fashion. "'Nuff for three," he growled.

Saxby lowered himself to the ground, grabbed the jug and drank deep; he gave a sigh of satisfaction as he put the jug down. "That shore is likker," he said reverently. "It hits right where I needed it."

Where you need to be hit is with an ounce of lead in yore belly, Rawhide thought, but out loud he said, "You shore took that like you know how to drink."

"Yeah, I kin drink — more'n most. I've drunk with some o th' hardest drinkin' characters in th' west an seen 'em all out. Now jus' to make shore I like this cornjuice . . . " He swung the jug up again and took another long pull at it — to Ben's obvious consternation.

"Here, give us a chance to drink level!" he growled, and almost snatched the jug from Saxby, who released it reluctantly and said,

"Ain't many as kin drink as much as me."

"Guess maybe you're quite a rider as well, huh? Usual fellers that kin drink kin ride too," Rawhide said.

"Ride? Me? Feller, I was top hand bronco buster at th' Slash Q in New Mexico, an' anyone that knows kin tell you what that means! Feller, I've shore forked some wild ones, been thrown all over creation at times, but I allus went back an' won, ain't never met th' hawss I couldn't beat." He clutched the jug again and took another pull at it, entirely disregarding the anguish on Ben's face. "An' poker — that's where I shine," he went on, with the least trace of thickening in his voice. "Cripes! I seen some games. 'Member one in El Paso — couple o' gamblers, railroad man, big rancher an' me, we played for forty-eight hours straight 'fore I cleaned 'em all out. Yessir! They all hadda holler 'nuff!"

"Ever been around a place called Hawksbee?" Rawhide asked, but as soon as he'd asked the question he saw caution gleam in Saxby's drink-clouded eyes and realised that he had been too previous.

"Hawksbee? Hawksbee? Seems to me I heard o' th' place, but I can't never call to mind havin' been there." Then he smiled derisively at Rawhide. "Said I could drink, didn't I?" he jeered, and Rawhide realised that Saxby knew what his object was.

"Shore you kin drink, 'n ride, 'n shoot, — an' talk."

"Yeah — but not too much."

"You kin shore talk yore way round wimmen, you smooth-tongued bastard!"

Saxby flushed and made a swiftly checked movement towards the gun he wasn't wearing.

"You've spoke some hard words to me, feller," he said, "but I'm forgivin' you — so far. Don' push me too hard. I ain't no slouch with a gun. Jus' 'cause I ain't wearin' one don' mean I can't use one!" Once again he swung the jug up to his lips and sucked down a long one. Ben took it as soon as it was back on the ground, had just got it to his lips when it was smashed out of his grip to break and spill its contents.

"You ol' sinner!" Mrs. Foran bawled at him. "You're leadin' these young fellers astray inta th' paths o' darkness an' sin. Strong drink is ragin' an' whisky's th' curse o' th' devil!"

Ben heaved himself up. "You dang ol' bitch!" he yelled at her. "You done wasted more'n pint o' good corn-liquor!"

"I ain't. I've saved you from th' edge o' destruction," she shouted back. "You're old enough an' wicked enough to know better! It's about time you started thinkin' 'bout th' next world 'stead o' leadin' young fellers on th' downward path."

"Gawd!" Ben exploded. "Downward path! Young fellers! Lemme tell you, you o' fool, that young feller there he drunk twice as much as me — I never had no chance! An' now you done spilt th' rest!"

"An' a good thing too — so much th' less temptation you gotta fight agin!" With that she tramped away back to the wagon, a blocky, determined figure.

"This here's yore fault!" Ben shouted at Rawhide. "If you hadn't had that dang fool idea o' makin' this feller drunk . . . "

"Oh, so that was th' idea, was it?" Saxby jeered. "Gonna make me drunk, huh? Feller, there ain't enough whisky in th' world to do that!"

And then at last Rawhide lost his temper. He lashed out at Saxby, smashed him full in the jaw and knocked him flat back into the fire. Instantly Marcia darted forward and dragged him out and dashed water over him. "You beast!" she shouted at Rawhide. "You beast! An' him still weak!"

Saxby wasn't badly burned; in a matter of minutes his smouldering clothes had been soused in water and he was sitting up again. Rawhide pulled Marcia to her feet. "Me an' you's gonna have a talk," he said. "Come away from here a piece."

"I won't! An' leave go of me, Storm!"

"Shut up for once an' do as I say. I've helped you some an' I reckon you owe me that."

"Yeah, maybe I do, but this ain't no time . . . "

"That's where you're wrong. I gotta talk to you."

"I ain't got nothin' to say to you an' I don' wanta lissen to nothin' you gotta say to me." She tried to pull her arm out of his grip, but failed.

"You're gonna lissen," he told her. "C'mon!"

Still she pulled back, so with a quick shift of his arms he picked her up, regardless of her kicking, struggling and squawking.

"Here, where are you takin' Marcia?" Mrs. Foran came tumbling down from the wagon like a pile of airtights overbalancing.

"Mind yore own dang business," Rawhide told her rudely, and pushed her aside as he stalked away into the darkness with Marcia in his arms.

He walked a hundred yards from the fire before he put her back on her feet when she promptly swung at his face. He caught her hand, picked her up again, turned her over and gave her a good spanking.

"There," he told her, when he released her. "There, maybe that'll maybe make you listen to sense!"

Almost she spat at him, beside herself with anger. "I ain't never been treated so. Western gentleman! Western bear! Beast! Bully!" She couldn't get the abuse out fast enough. He took her in his arms, covered her mouth with his and got a stinging slap in the face for his trouble; he gripped her shoulder and shook her until she was out of breath.

"Now you're gonna listen," he told her. "That feller — that Smith, he's Saxby, th' feller that stole my wife an' murdered her, th' feller that framed me for murder — an' killed yore pa, that's th' smooth-tongued jasper that's gotten you an' yore ma eatin' outa his hand, an' you too dumb to see it!"

"He ain't! He's jus' a feller that got lost in th' desert!"

"Aw, hell, Marcia! Be yore age!"

"I am. An' don't call me Marcia — I'm Miss Foran to you!"

"You're just a stupid kid in any language right now th' way you're behavin'. I don' want to see you tooken in by this lyin', oily-tongued cottonmouth."

"An' why should you worry about me?" Her tone was so sharply acid it brought him up short. Why, he wondered, was he worrying about her falling under the influence of Saxby?

Why should he waste a thought on her? All he had to do was shoot Saxby out of hand and pull his freight. He owed the Forans nothing. Already he had gone far out of his way to help them. Then, all of a sudden, he knew he loved her, knew that he had fallen in love with her back when he'd seen her the other side of Mountain City where their old wagon had stalled, and he knew in the same instant that somehow she had to be shown exactly what Saxby was.

"I'd worry about any decent gal I seen makin' a fool o' herself over that crook," he said lamely, for with the knowledge that he loved her had come the realisation that in trying to tell her exactly what Saxby was he was arousing her antagonism to him and increasing her prejudice in Saxby's favour.

"He ain't a crook," she told him. "He's just a cowpuncher makin' his way to Californy where he reckons he kin better himself an' git to own his own ranch."

"Him? Saxby? Git a ranch of his

own? Nuts! Don' make me laugh! I gotta split lip!"

"An' why shouldn't he git a ranch of his own?"

"'Cause he drinks or gambles every buck he earns an' he's so crooked you could screw him in th' floor." Too late, Rawhide saw he'd done the very thing he meant not to do; by talking Saxby down he had turned Marcia more than ever in his favour.

"You're against Smith for some reason," she said, "so I ain't gonna believe a word you say about him."

"Awright." Rawhide shrugged; he knew he'd gone about the thing in the wrong way, knew it was hopeless to try to convince her. "Awright, have it yore own way — but you'll learn, same as Alin did."

"Alin? Your wife?"

"Yeah. So what?"

"Why, nothin'. It's just that . . . "

"Nothin'. It ain't th' same feller — I was wrong. Forgit it. Let's git back to camp an' tell yore ma I ain't raped you like she thought I was gonna. C'mon!" He took her arm again to lead her back to camp, but she wrenched herself free.

"Take your han's offa me — you awready touched me too dang much. I see you for what you are, Storm, an' I don't like what I see. As for Californy, I guess we gotta travel together, but once we git there I ain't wantin' to see you again." With that she whirled round and ran towards the camp.

Rawhide followed her more slowly, furious with himself for having made such a mess of the talk but equally furious with Marcia for being such a fool over Saxby. Mrs. Foran was waiting for him and opened fire while he was still some distance away. He let her rant on until he was face to face with her, then — "Shut your dang yap!" he bawled. "'Member what I done to you in Mountain City? Awright, you keep quiet or I'll do it again!" She backed away a pace or two, for his furious tone of voice left no room for doubt that he meant what he said. She opened her mouth a couple of times but said nothing, before she sidled away to the wagon, apparently thoroughly cowed.

Rawhide slouched over towards Ben, spread his bedroll and lay down. However, it was some time before sleep came to him, for in the desert silence he could hear a mutter of conversation from the dimly lit wagon where, he had no doubt, Marcia and her mother were comparing notes to his detriment. Saxby had rolled into his blankets by the wagon and appeared to be asleep. Ben still sat staring into the fire, his jaws moving rhythmically over his quid. "Wimmen are plumb pizen," he said about an hour after Rawhide had turned in; he removed his quid, looked at the battered object with acute disfavour, then threw it in the fire before curling up under his blanket, his rifle held close to his chest. Rawhide took the hint, put his Colts inside his shirt; he didn't want to wake up looking into the muzzle of one of them held in Saxby's hand.

Breakfast next day was a dour, silent meal, enlivened by a passage at arms between Ben and Saxby, who apparently thought he had no work to do. "Go an' git them mules watered," Ben growled at him, "an' do it proper. We've got a hard day ahead an' we're gonna need all th' strength they got."

"Water yore own mules," Saxby growled back. "I ain't a teamster."

"Nor I ain't a servant!" Ben shouted; his temper was never at its best in the mornings. "I awready done too dang much for you — you ain't sick no more an' there ain't no reason why you shouldn't do some o' th' chores!"

Saxby got up, shrugged at Marcia and turned away towards the mules with a half wink at them as much as to say, 'See? I kin be nice even to such an ol' grouch.' Out loud he said, "Shore, I always figgered to pull my weight, but I don' savvy mules much."

"They kick," Rawhide told him as

he strolled away. "I'll help you with th' crocks," he told Marcia as she started to sluice them; for answer she just dropped them and walked away. Rawhide forced a grin. "Smart an' sassy," he commented. "Ben, way I figger it — I smell some around here!"

Ben bit a plug off his diminished stick of chewing, clamped it to shape before he said, "I figgered that too. Got any ideas?"

"Guess I might pull out — git on alone."

"An' this jasper you say is Saxby?"

"Could trail you, couldn't I?"

"We could. I ain't so set on actin' wet-nurse my ownself."

"You mean we both pull out?"

"Yeah, why not? They'll be in trouble soon enough."

"Yeah, an' then they'll find out jus' what a useless, two-timer skunk Saxby is."

"Gonna come hard on them wimmen."

"Shore, but will that worry you after that ol' bitch smashed yore jug?"

"She did, I know, but hell, Saxby or Smith — whoever he is — he don' know th' Journada. Maybe is as rider, but it ain't th' same thing, not none at all."

"He don' savvy nothin', but he's gotten a chrome streak a mile wide; it'll show purty soon an' they'll see him for what he is."

"Like I said — it ain't gonna be so good for them."

"We'll be around, Ben — he'll know that an' won't dare do no harm to 'em."

"No? I wouldn't bet on that. Still an' all, she did bust my jug, th' ol . . . Here he is now."

They turned and watched Saxby leading all eight mules towards the wagon. Rawhide grinned as he noticed that Saxby limped.

"Tol' you they kicked, didn't I?" he jeered.

Saxby just glared.

"You hitch up th' Foran's six an' leave mine be," Ben ordered.

"Six? Which six? An' why?"

"Why? 'Cause I'm dang well tellin' you. I ain't havin' my mules pullin' no waggin no further. Them las' two — you leave 'em alone!"

Ben clicked his lips and Joshua and Jezebel ambled towards him.

"I'll go saddle th' hawsses," Rawhide said, as he saw Mrs. Foran push her head out from under the tilt where she had been stowing gear; as he walked away he heard her ask:

"What you figgerin' to do, Ben? Ride today? Neither me nor Marcia drives good, you know!"

"Yeah, I know," Ben replied, "an' I'm ridin'. You'll hev to git yore fancy man to do th' drivin' — if he kin!"

"Shore I kin drive," Saxby boasted. "I been drivin' since I was six an' there ain't nothin' I don' know about it. But I figgered I'd ride today. Hey, Storm!"

Rawhide heard his shout, but went on cinching the saddle on Dancer as if he hadn't. As he pulled the last buckle tight he heard footsteps. "I don' remember tellin' you you could fork my cayuse, feller," Saxby told him.

"My cayuse. Remember? An' git outa my way — I need th' room!" He shoved Saxby aside as he went for the other saddle.

Saxby went red, shaped to swing over a punch, but was brought up short by the Colt that jumped into Rawhide's hand. "Git!" Rawhide told him. "Git! Make with th' feet! G'wan, spiel some more to them wimmen that are dang fools enough to believe you. Go on — pull yore freight!"

Saxby went, and Rawhide, after saddling the other horse, swung up into Dancer's saddle and rode back to the camp site where Ben was just finishing his diamond hitch on Jezebel's pack saddle. Marcia and Mrs. Foran had got down from the wagon. They looked worried and anxious. Saxby leant against the back of the vehicle, his eyes wary and cunning. "What's happening?" Mrs. Foran asked Ben as he cinched his riding saddle tight on Joshua's back. Rawhide eased Dancer to a stop, pushed his hat to the back of his head and smiled at her.

"We're pullin' out," he said sweetly.

"But you can't!" Marcia burst out. "You can't leave us!"

"Why not? This feller Saxby — or Smith if you say he is, he's High Jack and Big Casino. He knows it all, he does, he'll look after you far better'n us; we're jus' a couple o' roughnecks!"

"You can't mean this," Mrs. Foran almost pleaded. "We dunno th' way. We dunno . . . "

"You knew enough to bust my jug," Ben put in bitterly.

"I can't abide hard liquor, but that ain't no reason to leave us like this!"

Rawhide's face set hard. "Lady," he said, "speakin' personal, I can't think o' no reason at all why we shouldn't leave you. Me, I ain't popular — I'm learnin', anyhow. An' Ben . . . " He paused, his eyes upon Saxby, whose left arm had been thrust inside the wagon. Saxby brought his hand out empty and Rawhide went on, "Ben, he reckons he's got a right to have him a drink when he wants it."

"You're doin' this 'cause o' what I said last night," Marcia burst out, and as Rawhide turned his head to look at her Saxby's left hand dipped once more into the wagon and came out holding a shotgun.

"Git offa that hawss," he ordered harshly. "An' you, Ben, stop monkeying with that rifle! Git yore han's up, Storm!"

"I can't git offa bronc when I got my han's up round my ears," Rawhide answered equably. His eyes were on the shotgun and he was wondering whether it was loaded with buckshot or birdshot. At that range buckshot was lethal, birdshot no more than unpleasant. He looked narrowly at the shotgun. It must have been Foran's and it wasn't in very good shape, there was rust round the trigger guard, which meant that the triggers were almost certainly stiff; Rawhide reckoned he could draw and shoot at least as quickly as Saxby could fire the shotgun, but, strangely enough, he found he didn't particularly want to kill Saxby just then. He wanted Marcia and Mrs. Foran to find out about the man for themselves.

He lowered his hands a trifle, a movement followed instantly by the shotgun muzzles, then raked Dancer cruelly on the offside shoulder. The big horse, not expecting such treatment, spooked at once, buck-jumping so violently that Rawhide had to grab leather hurriedly, so nearly thrown he hardly heard the blast of the shotgun. Some of the birdshot pellets stung Dancer and he became unmanageable. Rawhide was only just able to stay with him as he exploded; he bucked, he sunfished, he swapped ends with a violence of which Rawhide had not believed him capable, finishing up by rearing vertically, then falling back on himself. Rawhide slid from the saddle just in time, swung back into the saddle as the horse got to his feet and stood still for a moment or two, trembling.

"Easy, feller," Rawhide soothed him, stroking his neck gently. "I know that weren't no way to treat a hawss, but I couldn't help it." Dancer blew, stamped a forefoot and, with that stamp, his burst of temper vanished.

Surprised to find how much ground the animal's acting up had covered, Rawhide turned his horse and rode back towards the camp where he found Ben, chewing steadily, holding a rifle on Saxby, whose hands were high. The empty shotgun lay at his feet and the expression on his face was not pleasant. Ben spat, shifted his rifle to the crook of his arm. "We ready now?" he asked.

Rawhide eased Dancer to a stop, patted his neck. "Guess so," he replied. "You reckon we oughta leave that jasper with a scatter-gun?"

"Might as well. He ain't dangerous — on'y stoopid."

"Then you really are leavin' us?" Marcia asked.

Rawhide looked at her straightly. "We're leavin'," he said. "We reckon you don' need us no more."

"But we don't know th' way!"

"Head for that gap in th' mountains," Ben told her. "That's Mosca Pass, there's water a couple o' miles past it — at Soda Lake. It ain't good water, so drink it careful. After that it's thirty-forty miles to Rock Springs an' from there you kin see th' Sierra Nevada. It ain't difficult. C'mon, Rawhide, we ain't got for ever!"

"Then you really are goin'?" Mrs. Foran demanded.

"Yeah. It's a free country, ain't it? An' I don' like havin' my likker spilt — I paid good money for thet jug." Ben kneed Joshua and, with Jezebel trailing behind, ambled out into the desert. Rawhide lifted one hand curtly to his hat and rode after Ben.

11

"HAD oughta be comin' soon." Ben turned his quid, spat, shifted his body fractionally but didn't answer Rawhide's remark, the first words that had passed between them for a couple of hours. The travelling had been as hard as ever that day, with long stretches of loose sand through which the animals, sinking fetlock deep, had only been able to plod wearily. The heat had been just as fierce out in the open, but it had been far worse when they reached Mosca Pass. This deep cleft took the trail through Mosca mountains and inside it the heat from the sun-scorched rocks was terrific; the three-mile length of the Pass had been torment for man and beast, an inferno of heat and choking dust. The almost sheer walls of the Pass were honeycombed with caves, caves in which the Apaches had been used to hide to ambush the wagon trains of years before, but Rawhide had been too hot and thirsty to spare more than a glance at the litter of grim relics which fringed the trail — the broken wagons, the bones of murdered immigrants, even the low mound where a small party of U.S. Cavalry had been cut down to the last man. Beyond the Pass the trail pitched steeply down for half a mile, then wound through a patch of stunted sand-blown willows and coarse sage which showed that there was water of a sort not very far below ground.

"Ain't no use diggin'," Ben had said, "th' water's mos'ly on'y alkali an' gives you th' gripes; we better git on to Soda Lake."

So they pushed on, although the water in their canteens had long been nothing but a memory, and the animals were in a bad state. An hour beyond the Pass, as they left the last willow sedge behind, Rawhide blinked and wiped an arm across his eyes, not daring to believe that what he saw wasn't a mirage, for there, before his eyes, appeared a lake, a silvery lake a couple of miles across.

Ben chuckled rustily. "It ain't a lake, but it ain't false water either," he said.

"Then what is it?"

"Salt."

"Salt? What th' hell you mean?"

"Jus' what I say — it's grass, see? But there's so much dang salt in th' ground it makes th' grass go silver. Looks mighty purty from a distance, don' it?"

"Is there water there?"

"Yeah — some, but it ain't good; we'll have to see th' mules an' hawsses don' drink much, gives them gripes too. But there's quail there. You never seen so many — pied quail, an' good eatin'."

"An' us with no shotgun."

"They're so tame you kin purty near pick 'em up."

Close to, the grass that had had the appearance of a lake looked like stubby spears of salt, and near the middle part of the salt grass water bubbled sluggardly up through a rock fault into a shallow pool; it was bitter to the taste, and brackish, but it was water.

Rawhide had never seen so many quail in his life. They were nearly as thick as snow on the ground and, as Ben said, were so tame they made little attempt to escape. Feeling rather as if he were a murderer, Rawhide caught half a dozen which were soon spitted and cooking over a near-smokeless fire Ben had built. With full bellies, their animals watered, they had withdrawn to the cover of a patch of mesquite and prickly pear which overlooked the water hole from a distance of perhaps half a mile. There they had lain for an hour, waiting for the arrival of the wagon.

"Don' reckon they turned back?" Rawhide asked after another pause.

Ben squinted up at the setting sun. "Not them," he replied, "that gal'll be trailin' this way for shore."

"Marcia? How'd you figger that?"

Ben chewed steadily for some minutes before he said, "'Cause she's nuts on you, feller!"

"You're crazy! She hates my guts!"

"That's where you're wrong, Rawhide; jus' 'cause she slapped yore face a couple o' times don' mean she hates you."

"But she does — she's fell for Saxby."

"Like hell she has! She jus' wants you to figger that way."

"Ben, I don' git this. If she don' like him why should she act th' way she does?"

"'Cause she's a woman, an' wimmen always goes by opposites. You been married — you oughta know that!"

"Then why'd she . . . ? Aw, hell, Ben, you can't be right!"

"Bet you I am — dang shore I am, 'cause here comes th' waggin!"

Rawhide soon afterwards saw what Ben's keener eyes had first perceived. They watched in silence as the Connestoga crept towards them; the six mules were pretty nearly beat out and only the smell of the water gave them strength to cover the last mile or two. Saxby sat slumped on the driving seat, but it was plain from his attitude that the progress of the wagon owed very little to his driving. At the water-hole he came to life, slammed the brake on, got down and lay at the pool drinking as if he had never drunk before. Marcia appeared, helped her mother down, scooped up water for her in a tin cup — even at that distance the watchers could see what wry faces the women made at the harsh taste of the water. When he had finished drinking, Saxby rolled over, sat up, built a cigarette and lit it. Rawhide's lips twisted in a sneer as he watched what happened; Marcia unhitched the mules and watered them one at a time while Mrs. Foran collected mesquite twigs and set about building a fire. It wasn't a very good fire, but Saxby made no attempt to help her; he just sat where he was on the ground. Marcia pulled it together and as darkness came down with desert abruptness the little point of light glowed redly, interrupted briefly as Mrs. Foran moved round it cooking the meal.

Rawhide watched with increasing restlessness, for he was becoming more and more sure that he had been wrong in leaving Marcia and her mother alone with Saxby. His unease increased as the meal ended and he saw Saxby lie back on the ground smoking, while the women did the chores.

"I'm going down," he told Ben, who only grunted.

Rawhide checked his guns, eased out from under his mesquite bush and began a slow, cautious approach to the camp; the salt-impregnated grass made most uncomfortable travelling, for unless handled with the utmost care it cut like a knife. The quail were made restless by his movement too, and since he had no wish to be greeted by a double charge of buckshot his progress was so slow that by the time he reached the dying fire the two women had climbed wearily back up into the wagon. As Rawhide reached the edge of the firelight Saxby got up, threw a few more sticks on the fire, then began to pace slowly up and down. Rawhide drew a Colt, lined it up; his target was clear, unmissable, yet he couldn't pull the trigger. He murmured an oath as he slid the weapon back into its holster and began to snake his way round the fire towards the wagon. As he neared it Saxby ceased his pacing and turned towards the wagon.

"Hey, Marcia! C'mon out here! I wanta talk with you!"

"I'm tired! An' anyway, I don' want to talk."

"C'mon out, I tell you! There's things I wanta say!"

"Say 'em some other time, young feller," Mrs. Foran told him sharply.

"We want some sleep — we had a hard day."

"What about me? I had a hard day too, drivin' them dang mules!"

"Yeah, maybe, but you ain't done a thing since . . . "

"Why should I? Cookin's women's work."

"Ben Simmonds didn't think so — nor Storm didn't. An' lookin' after mules ain't women's work!"

"No? Wa'al, I ain't doin' it nohow. I ain't a teamster!"

The wagon tilt opened and by the dim light of a candle Rawhide could see Mrs. Foran's stocky shape. She had the shotgun clutched in her hands. "Seems like you ain't any sort o' worker, Smith," she snapped. "Or maybe Storm was right, an' yore real name is Saxby!"

"Aw, you don' believe that, ma'am? How could I be th' sort of a jasper Storm talked about? I'm jus' a puncher aimin' to raise meself up by my bootstraps!"

"Well, jus' raise yoreself up by yore feet to th' other side o' that fire, an' remember it's our food you been eatin' an' our wagon you been ridin' on. Scat, an' quick! I kin use this gun!"

In the darkness Rawhide smiled as Saxby slouched away and rolled up in his blankets; he also smiled at the thought of Mrs. Foran turning gunwoman. While her husband had been alive she had been content to order him around, her authority based on a façade of illness, illness brought on by any prolonged resistance to her wishes. Now, with Foran dead, she was reaching deep to reserves of character with which to meet the situation into which she had thrust herself.

"Lazy good-for-nothin'," Rawhide heard her growl to Marcia. "Reckon Storm was maybe right."

"He don' look like a thief an' a murderer," Marcia answered.

"Murderers don' hardly ever do, Foran used to say. I ain't likin' this much, Marcia; reckon maybe I should ha' let Ben have his drunk out, but I jus' can't abide hard liquor."

"Maybe men that live hard need it."

"This is a strange country, but I ain't shore but what I couldn't git to like it if there was just a li'l more water. Did you drink much o' that stuff?"

"On'y what I had to. Ben said . . . "

"Yeah, an' I guess he was right. My stomach feels like it had a knot tied in it."

Rawhide moved quietly away; as he passed near Saxby he heard him groan, saw him roll out of his blankets and stagger away into the darkness — to the huge annoyance of the quail.

Having trouble suppressing his chuckles as he remembered how much water Saxby had drunk, Rawhide used the noise of the disturbed quail to make his way quickly back to Ben.

"They findin' out about him?" Ben queried.

"Looks like it. Miz Foran she shore

told him a piece — spoke up real plain."

"Uhuh. I figgered he didn't like work much. G'night." Ben was asleep and snoring inside a minute, but once again Rawhide had difficulty, for Ben's words about Marcia were rattling round in his brain like restless hail. He couldn't believe that Ben was right, and yet — yet she had kissed him back in Mountain City, and he was sure she wasn't the sort of girl to give her favours freely. Perhaps Ben had been right when he said she had favoured Saxby only because she liked Rawhide but didn't want to show it. "Danged if I know," he muttered, as he at last drifted off into a troubled sleep.

Soon after dawn the next morning, he and Ben watched while Saxby, evidently smarting under Mrs. Foran's rebuke, made leisurely preparations for breakfast. Nearly an hour passed before the meal was finished, the mules hitched and the wagon rolling slowly away westwards, an hour during which Rawhide and Ben fumed with impatience. Either of them could have completed the operation in less than half the time. Both wanted a drink and to water their own thirsty animals, which were being increasingly bothered by the particularly vicious and large brand of horse-fly which swarmed over Soda Lake and made a longer stay there impossible.

They waited until the Conestoga had at long last rolled over a swale of sand, hurried down to the hole, watered the mules and horses, cooked a quick meal over the remains of the fire Saxby had built.

"Shows he ain't no plainsman," Ben growled. "Lookit th' wood he's wasted; ain't much here anyways an' he has to use enough for three fires for one — an' that ain't even a good one!" The old man spat into the offending fire, then groaned as he got to his feet and lurched over to the spring to sluice his mug. "Gettin' old," he muttered, as much to himself as to Rawhide. "One more trip then I guess I'll haveta settle down. Maybe I'll strike it rich this time, could be I'll git married."

"Wouldn't want you for no step-pa-in-law," Rawhide told him.

"What me? Marry a woman that busts a jug o' liquor? Hell, no! You got me wrong, young feller. Why, I'd sooner tangle with a grizzly!"

"Suits me. Like I said, I wouldn't be wantin' no drunken ol' bum like you for a step-pa-in-law."

"I ain't no drunken ol' bum, dang you! I like a drink — shore, but I ain't never been drunk — not real drunk but about twenty times. Here, take this rope. I can't seem to git th' hitch right today."

The sun was well up before they left Soda Lake, and the heat already intense. Rawhide was beginning to get used to the discomfort by that time and was attaining the ability to withdraw into himself. The horses, however, were giving him increasing cause for worry; the poor feed, the bad water and, lastly, the vicious stings of the flies at Soda Lake had all combined to sap their strength, and as they pushed on across the dragging, clogging sand Rawhide found he had to change mounts with increasing frequency. Dancer was still in fair shape, but the horse he had got in Bristowe was about done. Ben's mules kept up surprisingly well, seemingly able to maintain their strength on the poor apology for feed they got. Progress was necessarily slow, and when the sun started to near the Sierra Nevada ahead of them they were still some miles from Rock Springs; they were also very thirsty, for the Soda Lake water had the disadvantage that it created nearly as much thirst as it quenched.

"We're gonna meet 'em at Rock Springs," Ben croaked. "Had figgered to swing around an' go past 'em, but they been makin' good time."

They had, once or twice during the day, sighted the wagon tilt as it crested a ridge of sand far ahead of them.

"Is it good water?" Rawhide asked.

"It ain't bad — not as bad as Soda Lake. On'y thing is there's snakes around there, 'most as many rattlers as there is quail at Soda Lake."

Rawhide muttered an oath. "This dang Journada is shore plumb dangerous; reckon I wouldn't never have gotten across without you, Ben."

"Nuts! Course you would. Been a bit harder, that's all, an' o' course jus' too bad effen you'd ha' missed out on any o' th' water holes."

"Seems like they all got somethin' wrong with 'em."

"All bar Ute Springs. That's good water. Say, there's Rock Springs but I don' see no wagon!"

They had just pitched over the crest of one of the eternal sand-heaves which made the desert so much a deception to anyone who thought it was level, and before them a long, fairly smooth stretch down to a small pool of water glinting red in the setting sun. The slope was rock-strewn and abounded in weirdly-shaped cactus; near the pool were some sizeable willows and some scrubby live oak. As Ben had said, there was no sign of the Conestoga and no vegetation large enough to hide it.

"Must ha' went on," Rawhide said.

"He didn't know we were behind 'em — shorely he figgered we're ahead?"

"C'mon Ben, I don' like this. There's somethin' I don't savvy; Saxby must ha' guessed I'd be waitin' for him th' first place in Californy; it ain't like him to push on."

"Maybe he seen us behind when we seen th' waggin?"

"Could be. Hell, Ben, there's some'un there — lyin' by th' pool! It's Marcia!" Rawhide roused Dancer to a shambling canter and hurried him to the pool, hurled himself out of the saddle beside the prone figure; it was not Marcia, but her mother stretched out unconscious, with a lump on the back of her head the size of a small quail.

Swearing furiously, Ben whipped his saddle off Joshua, and while Rawhide fetched water he propped her against the saddle as comfortably as possible. In a short while her eyelids fluttered up, but for a moment her eyes were blank, puzzled; then they cleared and she recognised Ben. At first she couldn't speak, but after she had had a drink she said, "You was right, an' I was wrong. He's all you said he was — an' more."

"What happened?" Ben asked, surprisingly gently for him.

"When we got here he left th' mules hitched an' let them drink; I didn't notice much. I hadn't been feelin' too good all day — I was worried. He filled th' water barranco'n then climbed back in th' wagon an' got Dad's shotgun. I tried to git it away from him, an' that's 'bout th' last thing I remember."

"Th' bastard!" Rawhide said softly. "An' he's gone off with Marcia!"

"How much of a start did he have, ma'am?" Ben asked.

Mrs. Foran looked doubtfully at the small rim of sun still showing over

263

the mountains. "'Bout two hours, I'd guess."

"An' th' mules — were they all fresh?"

"Didn't look too bad after they'd had a drink."

Ben scraped his chin. "There's some purty good feedin' for mules eight, ten miles further on," he muttered. "He could stop over there, rest up an' let 'em feed an' we'd never ketch him. I dunno!" He got up and walked slowly and stiffly towards Joshua who, having drunk, stood slack with weariness, cropping dispiritedly at the sparse grass. As Ben reached him there came a sharp, warning rattle, cut off short as the snake struck. Rawhide's hands flashed down on the instant, his Colt came out and up, roared, but too late the heavy bullet smashed the rattle snake's head to pulp. Ben, his face pale under the tan, was staring down at his thigh, where a tear in his overalls marked the place where the snake had struck. "Firs' time I ever been bit," he said weakly, and then collapsed.

Rawhide jumped at him, tore away the overalls, knelt and sucked at the twin punctures; he got some of the venom out and spat it into the sand, then he snatched his knife, gashed Ben's leg both above and below the bite. "An' us with no whisky!" he flung at Mrs. Foran. "We ain't got nothin' — thanks to you!"

"Git him up on his feet," she ordered. "He's gotta keep movin'."

"He ain't. We gotta stop the blood circulatin' all we can!" Rawhide snapped back at her. "An' stand away from him!" He bent once more, again sucked at the wound. Ben, breathing stertorously, had gone an unpleasant, bluish colour. "I ain't gonna let him die — I ain't," Rawhide muttered, then bent his head as Ben's eyes opened and the old man murmured:

"M'pack — gotta sack there — Injun snakebite stuff — but old . . . "

Rawhide ran to the pack, opened it out, scattering the contents, and found the embroidered bag which held only a few pinches of a whitish powder.

"You ain't gonna use that, are you?" Mrs. Foran demanded.

"Ain't got nothin' else, have I?" Rawhide answered her furiously, and poured the powder into the wound. He stood back and watched anxiously as Ben winced, then swore at the pain which was, in itself, a good sign, as he had at first appeared to have decided he was already as good as dead. In a matter of minutes he had turned a better colour; in a quarter of an hour he was sitting up and saying, "Dang good thing I minded that Injun stuff. Had it in my possibles for years an' never give it a thought."

"It's th' good Lord you ought to be thankin' — an' on yore knees," Mrs. Foran said severely, annoyed perhaps that her suggested remedy had been rejected. "It's Him that saved you an' not that horrible dirty ol' powder."

"It weren't you anyway," Ben blared at her. "If it weren't for you I'd ha' had me a good slug o' whisky an' never felt a thing! Hell, Rawhide. You needn't cut so deep!"

"Couldn't help it, ol' timer. That was a big rattler."

"I said there were plenty here, didn't I?"

"Lemme bind that wound for you," Mrs. Foran said. "You got a clean shirt or anythin'?"

Ben chuckled raspily. "Ain't had a clean shirt in years," he boasted. "This ol' buckskin's good enough for me — but there's a roll o' cloth in my pack."

She bustled away for it, thus missing the huge wink Rawhide gave Ben, who flushed angrily and used some oaths under his breath that wouldn't have pleased his would-be nurse. When she came back with some material he wriggled and grumbled so much as to make her task almost impossible. When at last it was done he heaved himself to his feet and moved his leg experimentally. "You oughta stay off that leg for a while," she warned.

"Git some sense, woman!" Ben grouched. "We gotta ketch that Saxby, an' we won't do that by sittin' around."

"An' we won't do it on Dancer," Rawhide said curtly. "He's played out, an' I ain't gonna ruin a good hawss."

"T'other?"

"Worse. Doubt if he'll ever be any good."

"Uhuh. Then, son, you better take Joshua."

"An' leave you?"

"Yeah. We can't all go. We'll rest up th' hawsses a piece an' then come on soon's we kin."

"Guess maybe that is th' way, but . . ."

"Ain't no 'buts'. You're th' one to go on. Make yoreself up enough food for a couple o' days — it's all you'll need. You'll be in Palo Seco by then an' gettin' a feed o' frijoles an' chile con carne — if you don't ketch up with them two first."

"I aim to," Rawhide said quietly as he began getting together a small supply of food which he packed in his bedroll; then he drank as much as he could, filled his canteen and swung into Joshua's saddle; after Dancer's height the mule felt ridiculous, but it seemed as strong as ever as he plodded away carrying Rawhide's weight.

12

IN the excitement of finding Mrs.
Foran at Rock Springs and the
subsequent flurry of Ben's snakebite,
Rawhide had forgotten that he was both
tired and hungry. Before he'd gone a
mile he wished he had taken time out
to eat — and drink afterwards. He ate
a little as he rode, but didn't dare eat
much because heat still radiated from
the sand and rocks and he wasn't
sure how far he would have to go
before he reached water. Joshua went
steadily, stubbornly on. Rawhide rocked
uncomfortably in the saddle, unused
to the awkward gait, half asleep with
weariness, half eager impatience to get
on. He knew it was no use trying
to hurry the mule, knew that at any
attempt to do so Joshua was quite
capable of stopping dead and refusing
to go on, so he swayed, slumped in the

saddle, oblivious of the array of stars overhead or the sharp, faint smell of the desert borne by the vagrant wind.

On and on, hour after hour, mile after mile, with the thought of Marcia ever present in his mind, Marcia and Saxby who had once again stolen a march on him. Ceaselessly his brain reviewed the actions he had taken during his long chase, again and again he tried to reassure himself that he had been right to do as he had done; he was particularly unsure about having left the party at Ute Springs. If he hadn't — he shook his head wearily for the dozenth time and tried to make himself think of nothing else but the trail ahead, the wagon tracks clear under the starlight.

After three hours he came upon better ground, the sand and rock scattered with sparse bunch grass, the trend of the land was upwards and above him he sensed rather than saw the loom of the Sierra.

Cactus and yucca grew thickly, and

soon he smelt the bitter-sweet scent of sage. The trail steepened and, as Joshua stumbled for the first time, he saw a red glow about two miles ahead. Nearly an hour it took him to reach it, for although the mule was ready to go on till he dropped, his strength was almost exhausted, sapped all the more quickly by the steepening grade. The glow was that of a fire — a fire that was dying down, a fire which had fed upon the Conestoga he had found in Mountain City. The moon had risen and by its light Rawhide saw what had happened. The trail wound its way up round the shoulder of a foothill; Saxby, if he had been driving, had gone too near the edge, which had crumbled under the wagon's weight. It hadn't rolled far, however, only thirty or forty feet, before being brought up against an outcrop of rock, but even from the embers Rawhide could see it had been smashed beyond repair.

He tied Joshua to a stunted jack-pine and clambered down the slope, fear for

Marcia gripping his heart. He found one dead mule thrown some distance from the wagon; another close by, which had been shot, that was all — unless, and he refused to believe it, unless Marcia's body was there, burnt to ashes in the middle of the fire. If she'd gone on with Saxby they still had four mules, he thought grimly as he clambered back up to the trail and found Joshua lying down. Nothing he could do would get Joshua to his feet. Rawhide kicked him, pleaded, swore, but not a movement would the mule make. There was a stubborn, resigned look in his eyes which said quite clearly, "This is as far as I carry you — I've done enough and I'm doing no more."

After a quarter of an hour's wasted effort, Rawhide shrugged fatalistically, took his canteen and such food from his bedroll as he reckoned he could carry, and started to walk. He was tired already, the trail was steep and rough underfoot, his boots hopelessly unsuitable for walking. Soon existence became for him merely a matter of swinging one foot forward hoping the foot wouldn't turn on a stone, transferring his weight, then doing the same with the other leg. Now and again he fell, and soon the dust which his feet kicked up caked with blood as well as sweat. Time passed, but still the moonlit slope above him seemed to stretch as far as ever, to go on rising interminably towards the sky. He was so near the ragged edge of exhaustion near dawn that when at last the trail stopped rising he did not at first realise it, in fact he fell again because he lifted one foot too high, overbalancing when it did not meet the expected resistance.

For some minutes he lay in the dust where he had fallen, too dazed and tired to move, then behind him the horizon glowed with light and he knew that the day which was coming would see the end of his long chase. Why or how he knew he couldn't have explained, but he knew it as certainly as he knew he was close to collapse with thirst and fatigue. He drank what little water remained in his canteen, ate a little food, built and smoked a cigarette. As he struggled to his feet and lurched on, the rest didn't seem to have done him any good; he was more uncertain than ever, and even though the trail was now downhill it was more and more difficult to go on pushing one foot before the other. But he shuffled on and on, only vaguely conscious that he was no longer in the desert country; good bunch grass covered the slopes, tree clumps gave promise of water, although he was too far gone to realise it.

Right foot forward, left foot forward, each movement required a definite order from his brain. He kept moving, though his progress was painfully slow, kept moving, conscious only of the trail stretching in front of him. On and on, on and on until, surprisingly, something blocked the trail, something solid into which he bumped, from which he rebounded, falling helplessly backward into the dust.

Slowly, painfully slowly, he managed to sit up and saw that he sat in the middle of a wide street flanked on either side by shabby, red-tiled adobe buildings. He also saw that the object which had stopped his progress was a large man from whose belly he had rebounded.

"Git outa my way," he croaked. "I'm lookin' for a feller."

The large man, who wore a sheriff's star and a puzzled expression, said, "So'm I, I'm looking for you, feller. C'mon to th' jail, will you?"

"Jail? What for?"

"You're Saxby, I'd guess — an' wanted for murder!"

"Saxby?" At first Rawhide's weary brain couldn't absorb the meaning of the sheriff's words, but as that meaning penetrated he laughed hysterically. "Saxby?" he croaked. "I ain't Saxby, you dang fool! I'm lookin' for him!"

"That's what he said you'd say. C'mon, jail, you!"

The sheriff bent suddenly and took Rawhide's guns, then jerked him to his feet. "We been lookin' for you for quite some time," he said as his grip on Rawhide's arm tightened and he led him towards one of the adobe buildings which a warped and faded sign stated was — 'County Jail.'

Inside the thick adobe walls the building was cool and pleasantly dim after the glare outside. The sheriff deposited his prisoner in a chair, then got a bottle and glasses out of his desk. "Maybe you are a murderer," he said, "but you look like you need a drink. Water chaser?"

He filled a tumbler with cool water from a sweating olla and gave it to Rawhide with a full whisky glass. Rawhide drank gratefully, then for the first time he looked carefully at his captor. "Elmer Daniels! It ain't! It can't be!"

"You ain't Storm — Rawhide Storm,

used to be bunkies with me in Nucces?"

Rawhide laughed rustily, weak with relief as he realised that at long last Saxby's luck had broken.

"Yeah, it's me awright, ol' timer. An' now maybe you'll believe me when I tell you I ain't Saxby."

"Yeah, shore. But who'n hell is this Saxby?"

"Feller I been chasin' for months, framed me for murder an' then . . . Blazes, Elmer! It'd take all day to tell you all I got on that sidewinder. What I wanta know is where is he now?"

The sheriff stared at his old friend and poured him another drink.

"Coach," he said curtly. "Pulled out at noon, half an hour ago. But easy, feller. Easy." He pushed Rawhide back into the chair from which he had started to struggle up.

"Nuts, Elmer! I gotta git after him, he's got Marcia . . . "

"That gal, huh? She looked played

out an' kinda scared, didn't say nothin'."

"She didn't dare. Hell, man! I gotta git. I need a hawss."

"Awright, awright, Rawhide, take yore time — we got plenty."

"Plenty my foot! That bastard's got a head start. Lemme up, Elmer!"

"You set right where you are — an' take another drink, we got plenty o' time. You need food — an' a clean-up, maybe an hour's sleep."

"Are you nuts, Elmer? He's gittin' away, man! He's gittin' away!"

"Not far, he ain't. Stage road swings south from here, takes in Aguas Frias an' then has to swing north agin along th' valley. There's a trail across from here — bad, but not too bad. We kin do it easy in an hour to San Pedro. Coach ain't due there till five. Relax, feller!"

Rawhide slumped back in his chair. Now that the urgency of pursuit was gone the brief thorn fire of his energy burnt out quickly; once more he was desperately weary, hardly able to keep his eyes open.

The sheriff looked at him shrewdly, eased him over to a bunk. "Hour's sleep'll put you right," he said. "Pound yore ear for a spell. I'll git food an' hawsses organised."

Rawhide was asleep before the sheriff had finished, and when, an hour later, the law officer shook him he awoke feeling surprisingly refreshed, sluiced his face and hands before wolfing down the meal Elmer had sent in.

"So Saxby tol' you to be waitin' for me, huh?" he asked, as he spooned sugar into his coffee.

"Yeah. Shore tol' me some about you; said there was a ten-thousan' buck reward out for you — an' I could use ten grand." The sheriff paused, then went on, "He sold them mules, rested up a bit an' then caught th' stage."

"An' Marcia didn't say nothin'?"

"Nary a word. She looked like she was in some kind of a daze. An' yeah, 'nother thing — this feller bought himself a pair o' Colts from ol' Austin, good pair too."

"Uhuh. Heeled now, is he? Awright, let's go, Elmer!"

It was a relief to be on a horse again after the jolting mule, and though, as Daniels had warned, the trail was rough it was easy compared with the Journada. After little over an hour's riding they had crossed a spine of the Sierra and were tying their horses in a cottonwood clump which looked down upon the stage road. To his surprise, Rawhide was icy calm; he checked his guns in as matter-of-fact-way as if he were going to shoot jack-rabbits. Daniels pulled out a huge old watch.

"'Bout half an hour," he said quietly, before pushing the timepiece back and reaching for his tobacco sack. "How'd you like th' Journada?"

"Didn't — not none at all. It's bad travellin'."

"Ain't many uses it now."

"I ain't surprised. 'Minds me, there's a friend o' mine comin' along behind — ol' prospector an' Marcia's ma. I hadda leave 'em at Rock Springs where Saxby ditched her."

"Right nice feller, huh?"

"Oh, shore."

They chatted idly, going over what had happened to each of them in the years since they'd last met, until Daniels said, "Here she comes — right on time. Ol' Tom's due for a shock!" He ground out his cigarette butt, untied his horse and swung heavily up into the saddle, grumbling as he did so. "Don' ride as light as I used to," he lamented. "It's all this dang Spanish food — I like it too much."

As Rawhide mounted he saw the old Concord coach rolling along fast behind its six-horse team, dust billowing in a cloud behind it; half a mile, quarter of a mile, fifty yards, then Daniels kicked his horse out from among the trees and bawled out, "Hold up, Tom! Hold up!"

After that things happened fast. The driver slammed on his brake, pulled his horses up, the dust cloud catching up as the coach slowed, obscuring Rawhide's view as he rode out. He saw a face at the coach window and heard the blast of a shot as he slid out of his saddle. He ran forward, pulling a gun; there was another shot as he wrenched at the door, Marcia screaming, Saxby cursing. Rawhide was dimly aware that she was struggling with Saxby and trying to get the Colt out of his hand, the Colt that, as the door cracked open, was pointing at Rawhide. He saw flame blossom from the muzzle and was aware that a great weight struck his head and then, as the ground came up to meet him, he heard the blast of yet another shot.

Rawhide wasn't out for long and came to with his head in Marcia's lap, with Marcia wiping blood from a gash ploughed across his head by Saxby's bullet, with Marcia's tears falling on his face.

"Saxby?" he whispered.

"Dead," Marcia gulped. "I — I shot

him. I — I — you were right about him, Rawhide, an' I — I was terribly wrong."

"Knew you'd find out," he replied comfortably. "An' now you better kiss me."

THE END

Other titles in the Linford Western Library:

TOP HAND
Wade Everett

The Broken T was big. But no ranch is big enough to let a man hide from himself.

GUN WOLVES OF LOBO BASIN
Lee Floren

The Feud was a blood debt. When Smoke Talbot found the outlaws who gunned down his folks he aimed to nail their hide to the barn door.

SHOTGUN SHARKEY
Marshall Grover

The westbound coach carrying the indomitable Larry and Stretch headed for a shooting showdown.

DONOVAN
Elmer Kelton

Donovan was supposed to be dead. Uncle Joe Vickers had fired off both barrels of a shotgun into the vicious outlaw's face as he was escaping from jail. Now Uncle Joe had been shot — in just the same way.

CODE OF THE GUN
Gordon D. Shirreffs

MacLean came riding home, with saddle tramp written all over him, but sewn in his shirt-lining was an Arizona Ranger's star.

GAMBLER'S GUN LUCK
Brett Austen

Gamblers seldom live long. Parker was a hell of a gambler. It was his life — or his death . . .

SUNDANCE: SILENT ENEMY
John Benteen

A lone crazed Cheyenne was on a personal war path. They needed to pit one man against one crazed Indian. That man was Sundance.

LASSITER
Jack Slade

Lassiter wasn't the kind of man to listen to reason. Cross him once and he'll hold a grudge for years to come — if he let you live that long.

LAST STAGE TO GOMORRAH
Barry Cord

Jeff Carter, tough ex-riverboat gambler, now had himself a horse ranch that kept him free from gunfights and card games. Until Sturvesant of Wells Fargo showed up.

WOLF DOG RANGE
Lee Floren

Will Ardery would stop at nothing, unless something stopped him first — like a bullet from Pete Manly's gun.

DEVIL'S DINERO
Marshall Grover

Plagued by remorse, a rich old reprobate hired the Texas Trouble-shooters to deliver a fortune in greenbacks to each of his victims.

GUNS OF FURY
Ernest Haycox

Dane Starr, alias Dan Smith, wanted to close the door on his past and hang up his guns, but people wouldn't let him.

BRETT RANDALL, GAMBLER
E. B. Mann

Larry Day had the choice of running away from the law or of assuming a dead man's place. No matter what he decided he was bound to end up dead.

THE GUNSHARP
William R. Cox

The Eggerleys weren't very smart. They trained their sights on Will Carney and Arizona's biggest blood bath began.

THE DEPUTY OF SAN RIANO
Lawrence A. Keating and
Al. P. Nelson

When a man fell dead from his horse, Ed Grant was spotted riding away from the scene. The deputy sheriff rode out after him and came up against everything from gunfire to dynamite.

FARGO: PANAMA GOLD
John Benteen

With foreign money behind him, Buckner was going to destroy the Panama Canal before it could be completed. Fargo's job was to stop Buckner.

FARGO:
THE SHARPSHOOTERS
John Benteen

The Canfield clan, thirty strong were raising hell in Texas. Fargo was tough enough to hold his own against the whole clan.

PISTOL LAW
Paul Evan Lehman

Lance Jones came back to Mustang for just one thing — revenge! Revenge on the people who had him thrown in jail.

FIGHTING RAMROD
Charles N. Heckelmann

Most men would have cut their losses, but Frazer counted the bullets in his guns and said he'd soak the range in blood before he'd give up another inch of what was his.

LONE GUN
Eric Allen

Smoke Blackbird had been away too long. The Lequires had seized the Blackbird farm, forcing the Indians and settlers off, and no one seemed willing to fight! He had to fight alone.

THE THIRD RIDER
Barry Cord

Mel Rawlins wasn't going to let anything stand in his way. His father was murdered, his two brothers gone. Now Mel rode for vengeance.

RIFLES ON THE RANGE
Lee Floren

Doc Mike and the farmer stood there alone between Smith and Watson. There was this moment of stillness, and then the roar would start. And somebody would die . . .

HARTIGAN
Marshall Grover

Hartigan had come to Cornerstone to die. He chose the time and the place, and Main Street became a battlefield.

SUNDANCE: OVERKILL
John Benteen

When a wealthy banker's daughter was kidnapped by the Cheyenne, he offered Sundance $10,000 to rescue the girl.

GUNSLINGER'S RANGE
Jackson Cole

Three escaped convicts are out for revenge. They won't rest until they put a bullet through the head of the dirty snake who locked them behind bars.

RUSTLER'S TRAIL
Lee Floren

Jim Carlin knew he would have to stand up and fight because he had staked his claim right in the middle of Big Ike Outland's best grass.

THE TRUTH ABOUT SNAKE RIDGE
Marshall Grover

The troubleshooters came to San Cristobal to help the needy. For Larry and Stretch the turmoil began with a brawl and then an ambush.

ARIZONA DRIFTERS
W. C. Tuttle

When drifting Dutton and Lonnie Steelman decide to become partners they find that they have a common enemy in the formidable Thurston brothers.

TOMBSTONE
Matt Braun

Wells Fargo paid Luke Starbuck to outgun the silver-thieving stagecoach gang at Tombstone. Before long Luke can see the only thing bearing fruit in this eldorado will be the gallows tree.

HIGH BORDER RIDERS
Lee Floren

Buckshot McKee and Tortilla Joe cut the trail of a border tough who was running Mexican beef into Texas. They stopped the smuggler in his tracks.

ORPHAN'S PREFERRED
Jim Miller

Sean Callahan answers the call of the Pony Express and fights Indians and outlaws to get the mail through.

DAY OF THE BUZZARD
T. V. Olsen

All Val Penmark cared about was getting the men who killed his wife.

THE MANHUNTER
Gordon D. Shirreffs

Lee Kershaw knew that every Rurale in the territory was on the lookout for him. But the offer of $5,000 in gold to find five small pieces of leather was too good to turn down.

FARGO: MASSACRE RIVER
John Benteen

The ambushers up ahead had now blocked the road. Fargo's convoy was a jumble, a perfect target for the insurgents' weapons!

SUNDANCE: DEATH IN THE LAVA
John Benteen

The Modoc's captured the wagon train and its cargo of gold. But now the halfbreed they called Sundance was going after it . . .

HARSH RECKONING
Phil Ketchum

Five years of keeping himself alive in a brutal prison had made Brand tough and careless about who he gunned down . . .